She just about
touch.

"Lucy...stop."

She didn't move her hand. "I can't."

He couldn't have moved away if he'd tried. She was pure temptation. And he wanted her.

When he dipped his head, his intention clear, a tiny moan escaped her. It was the sweetest kiss he'd ever experienced, almost as though it possessed a kind of purity that had never been matched and never would.

Brant suddenly felt as if he'd been sucker-punched. Because he'd known, deep down, that kissing Lucy would be incredible. Everything about her had been tempting him for months. Every look, every word, every touch had been drawing them toward this moment. His pulse galloped, knees grew weak, until he pulled back and looked into those honest eyes.

What was he doing? Lucy was the hometown girl who wanted romance, marriage, the white picket fence. Brant didn't do any of those things.

Her eyes shimmered with a kind of longing that heated his blood even further. But he fought the urge to kiss her again, because he knew where it would lead. He'd want to make love to her forever... and that was the one thing he couldn't give.

CEDAR RIVER COWBOYS:
Riding into town with romance on their minds!

Dear Reader,

Welcome back to Cedar River, South Dakota!

Also welcome to my ninth book for Harlequin Special Edition, *Lucy & the Lieutenant*.

I wanted to write a book about unrequited love. About that girl many of us have been...that girl who loves a boy from afar, never quite having the courage to let him know.

Lucy Monero is a kind, hardworking small-town doctor. Without any family of her own, she cares deeply for her patients and her small group of friends. She also cares for Brant Parker. In fact, Lucy's been in love with him since she was fifteen. But since the ex-soldier has always treated her like she's invisible, Lucy knows she has to get any romantic ideas of Brant out of her system once and for all. Which is easier said than done since his elderly uncle is one of her patients.

Brant has no intention of getting involved with Lucy Monero, despite his mother's matchmaking efforts or the fact he runs into her at every turn! The pretty brunette invades his thoughts way too often. Since leaving the military, though, he's not in the market for a serious relationship, especially not with someone as pure and hometown as Lucy. He's seen too much, been through too much. But he quickly discovers that what he wants isn't necessarily what he needs.

I hope you enjoy *Lucy & the Lieutenant* and I'd like to invite you back to Cedar River very soon for my next book, Brooke and Tyler's story!

I adore hearing from readers and can be reached by email, Twitter and Facebook, or sign up for my newsletter via my website, helenlacey.com. Please visit anytime as I love talking about my pets, my horses and, of course, cowboys. I'll also share news about upcoming books in my latest series for Special Edition, The Cedar River Cowboys!

Warmest wishes,

Helen Lacey

Lucy & the Lieutenant

Helen Lacey

978-0-373-65964-7

Lucy & the Lieutenant

This edition published by arrangement with Harlequin Books S.A.

For questions and comments about the quality of this book, please contact us at CustomerService@Harlequin.com.

Printed in U.S.A.

Helen Lacey grew up reading *Black Beauty* and *Little House on the Prairie*. These childhood classics inspired her to write her first book when she was seven, a story about a girl and her horse. She loves writing for Harlequin Special Edition, where she can create strong heroes with a soft heart and heroines with gumption who get their happily-ever-after. For more about Helen, visit her website, helenlacey.com.

Books by Helen Lacey

Harlequin Special Edition

The Cedar River Cowboys

Three Reasons to Wed

The Prestons of Crystal Point

The CEO's Baby Surprise

Claiming His Brother's Baby
Once Upon a Bride
Date with Destiny
His-and-Hers Family
Marriage Under the Mistletoe
Made for Marriage

Visit the Author Profile page
at Harlequin.com for more titles.

For Robert...to the moon and back.

Chapter One

Brant Parker grabbed the T-shirt stuffed in the back pocket of his jeans and wiped his brow.

It was cold out, but he'd been working for four hours straight without a break and it was quite warm inside the closed-up rooms of the Loose Moose Tavern. He'd spent the best part of three weeks stripping out the old timber framing and flooring that had gone through a fire eight months earlier.

Most people said he was crazy for buying the place, like it had some kind of hoodoo attached to it. But he didn't believe in hoodoo or bad luck, and he wasn't swayed by anyone telling him what he should or shouldn't do. The Loose Moose had been a part of Cedar River for over thirty years and he believed the old place deserved another chance.

Maybe he did, too.

Brant dropped the piece of timber in his hands,

stretched his back and groaned. It had been a long day and he wanted nothing more than to soak under a hot shower and to relax in front of some mindless TV show for an hour or two. But first he had to go to the veterans home to visit his uncle, as he did every Tuesday and Friday.

Uncle Joe was his father's oldest brother and a Vietnam veteran who'd lost a leg in the war. He also had a heart condition and suffered from the early stages of Parkinson's disease. He lived in full-time care at the home adjacent to the small community hospital. Brant cared deeply for his uncle. The older man knew him. Got him. Understood the demons he carried.

He headed upstairs to the small apartment and took a shower, then dressed in jeans and a long-sleeved shirt. It was snowing lightly, a regular occurrence in South Dakota in winter, but quite unusual for mid-November. He shouldered into his lined jacket, pulled on woolen socks and heavy boots, and grabbed his truck keys. The home was a ten-minute drive in good weather from the main street in town and since snow was now falling in earnest, he knew the roads would be slippery. Brant took his time and arrived about fifteen minutes later. It was late afternoon and the parking lot was empty, so he scored a spot easily and got out of the truck.

The wind howled through his ears and he pulled the jacket collar around his neck. It promised to be a long and chilly winter ahead. But he didn't mind. It sure beat the relentless, unforgiving heat of a desert summer like the last one he'd endured in Afghanistan. The light blanket of snow made him feel as though he was home. And he was. For good this time. No more tours. No more military. He was a civilian and could lead a normal life. He could get up each morning and face a new day. And he could forget everything else.

Brant headed for the front doors and shook off his jacket before he crossed the threshold. When he entered the building, heat blasted through him immediately. The foyer was empty and the reception desk had a sign and a bell instructing to ring for attendance. He ignored both and began walking down the wide corridor.

"Hi, Brant."

The sound of his name stopped Brant in his tracks and he turned. A woman emerged from a door to his left and he recognized her immediately. *Lucy Monero.* He cringed inwardly. He wasn't in the mood for the pretty brunette with the lovely curves and dancing green eyes, and tried to stay as indifferent as possible. "Good afternoon, Dr. Monero."

"Please," she said just a little too breathlessly. "Call me Lucy."

He wouldn't. Keeping it formal meant keeping her at a distance. Just as he liked it.

Instead he made a kind of half-grunting sound and shrugged loosely. "Have you seen my uncle this afternoon?"

"Just left him about ten minutes ago," she said, smiling. "He said he's feeling good today. The nurses left food on the tray, so perhaps see if you can get him to eat something."

"Sure."

She didn't move. Didn't pass. She simply stood there and looked at him. Examined him, he thought. In a way that stirred his blood. It had been too long since anything or anyone had stirred him. But Lucy Monero managed it with barely a glance.

And he was pretty sure she knew it.

"So, how's the shoulder?" she asked, tossing her hair in a way that always made him flinch.

A trace of her apple-scented shampoo clung to the air and he swallowed hard. "Fine."

He'd dislocated his shoulder eight weeks earlier when he'd fallen off his motorbike. She'd been one of the doctors on duty at the hospital that night. But he'd made a point of ensuring she didn't attend him. He hadn't wanted her poking and prodding at him, or standing so close he'd be forced to inhale the scent of her perfume.

"Glad to hear it. I was talking to your mother the other day and she said you plan to reopen the tavern in the next few months?"

His mother had made her opinion about Lucy Monero clear on numerous occasions. She was Lucy's number-one fan and didn't mind telling him so. But he wasn't interested in a date, a relationship or settling down. Not with anyone. Including the pretty doctor in front of him. Her dark brows and green eyes were a striking combination and no doubt a legacy from her Italian heritage. She wore scrubs with a white coat over them, and he figured she'd just come from the emergency room at the hospital where she worked. But he knew she was also filling in at the veterans home a couple of times a week while one of the other doctors was on leave. Uncle Joe thought the world of her, too. And even his older brother, Grady, had extolled her virtues after she'd attended to his youngest daughter when the child had been taken to the ER a couple of months ago with a high fever.

Brant did his best to ignore her eyes, her hair and the curves he knew were hidden beneath the regulation blue scrubs. "That's the plan."

She smiled a little, as though she was amused by his

terse response, as though she had some great secret only she was privy to. It irritated him no end.

"I'm pleased your shoulder is okay."

He wished she'd stop talking. "Sure, whatever."

Her eyes sparkled. "Well, see you soon, Brant."

She said his name on a sigh. Or at least, that's how it sounded. There was a husky softness to her voice that was impossible to ignore. And it *always* made him tense. It made him wonder how her voice would sound if she was whispering, if she was bent close and speaking words only he could hear.

Brant quickly pulled himself out of the haze his mind was in and nodded vaguely, walking away, well aware that she was watching him.

And knowing there wasn't a damned thing he could do about.

Lucy let out a long sigh once Brant Parker disappeared around the corner of the ward. His tight-shouldered gait was one she would recognize anywhere—at the hospital, along the street, in her dreams.

He'd been in them for years. Since she'd been a starry-eyed, twelve-year-old mooning over the then-fifteen-year-old Brant. She'd lived next door to the Parker ranch. The ranch he'd left when he was eighteen to join the military. She'd left Cedar River for college just a couple of years later and put the boy she'd pined over as a teen out of her thoughts. Until she'd returned to her hometown to take a position at the small county hospital. She'd seen him again and the old attraction had resurfaced. He had been back from another tour of the Middle East and they'd bumped into each other at the O'Sullivan pub. Of course he hadn't recognized her. The last time they'd crossed paths she had been a chubby, self-conscious teenager with glasses. He'd seemed surprised to see her, but had said little. That had been more than two years earlier. Now he was back for good. Just as she was. He had left the military after twelve years of service and bought the old Loose Moose Tavern.

He could have done anything after high school—maybe law or economics—as he was supersmart and was always at the top of his class. One of those gifted people who never had to try hard to make good grades. He spoke a couple of languages and had been some kind of covert translator in the military. Lucy didn't know much about it, but what she did she'd learned from his mother, Colleen. The other woman regularly visited Joe Parker and also volunteered at the hospital where Lucy specialized in emergency medicine.

She'd known the Parkers since she was a child. Back then her parents had owned the small ranch next door. When she was fourteen her dad had died unexpectedly from a stroke, and then within a year her mother had sold the place and moved into town. A few years later her mother was killed in an accident. By then Lucy was ready for college, which would be followed by medical school, and had left town. The house her mother had bought in town was now hers and it was conveniently located just a few streets from the hospital. She was back in Cedar River to give back to the town she loved.

And maybe find her own happiness along the way.

Because Lucy wanted to get married and have a family. And soon. She was twenty-seven years old and had never had a serious romantic relationship. She'd never been in love. The truth be told, she'd never really been kissed.

And she was the only twenty-seven-year-old virgin she knew.

In high school she had been a geek to the core and had mostly been ignored by the boys in her grade. She hadn't even managed to get a date for prom. And by the time she was in college, her dreams about dating quickly disappeared. Three weeks into college and her roommate was assaulted so badly Lucy spent two days with the other girl at the hospital. It was enough to make her wary about getting involved with anyone on campus. She made a few friends who were much like herself—focused kids who studied hard and avoided parties and dating. By the time she started medical school the pattern of her life had been set. She was quiet and studious and determined to become a good doctor. Nothing else mattered. Though she'd gotten more comfortable over time in social situations, she was known as a girl who didn't date and, after a while, the invitations stopped.

One year quickly slipped into another and by the time she'd finished her residency she'd stopped fretting about being the oldest virgin on the planet. Not that she was hanging on to it as though it was a prize…she'd just never met anyone she liked enough to share that kind of intimacy with. Of course her closest friends, Ash, Brooke and Kayla, thought it amusing and teased her often about her refusal to settle for just *anyone*. She wanted special. She wanted a love that would last a lifetime.

She wanted…

Brant Parker.

Which was plain old, outright, what-are-you-thinking-girl stupid, and she knew it deep within her bones. Brant never looked at her in that way. Most of the time he acted as though he barely even *saw* her. When they were kids he'd tolerated her because they were neighbors, and in high school he had been three years ahead and hadn't wasted his time acknowledging her in the corridors. By the time she was in college he was long gone from Cedar River.

Her cell beeped and quickly cut through her thoughts. It was Kayla reminding her that she'd agreed to meet her and Ash and Brooke at the O'Sullivan pub for a drink and catch-up that evening. It had become something of a Friday-night ritual since she'd returned to town. Kayla had been a friend since junior high and worked as curator of the small Cedar River historical museum and art gallery, and Ash was a cop with the local police department. Brooke, who was Brant's cousin, was pure cowgirl and owned a small horse ranch just out of town.

All four women were good friends and she thoroughly enjoyed their company…most of the time. But she wasn't really in the mood for drinks and conversation tonight. She'd had a long morning in the emergency room and had been at the veterans home for the past few hours. She was tired and wanted nothing more than to go home, strip off and soak in the tub for a leisurely hour or so. But since her friend wouldn't take no for an answer, she agreed to meet them at the pub at six, which gave her an hour to get home, feed the cat, shower and change, and then head back into town.

Lucy ended the call and walked toward the nurses' station. She handed in her charts to the one nurse on duty and signed out. She had another two weeks at the home before her contract was up and then she'd return full-time to the hospital. But she'd enjoyed her time working with the veterans. And with Joe Parker in particular. He was a natural storyteller and entertained everyone with his charm and easy-going manner.

Pity his nephew didn't inherit some of those manners or charm.

Lucy wrinkled her nose and headed down the hall to

the small locker room. Brant made her mad the way he ignored her. It wasn't like he was some great catch or anything. Sure, he had a body to die for. And the sexiest deep blue eyes. And dark hair that she'd often imagined running her fingers through. But he was a moody, closed-off loner who didn't seem to have time for anyone. Except his closest family members. She'd seen him in town one morning with his young nieces and the girls clearly adored him. It had made her think about how he'd probably make a great dad one day. And the idea of that quickly had her womb doing backflips.

Idiot...

She shrugged off her foolish thoughts, hung up her white coat and grabbed her bag.

The cold air outside hit her like a laser blast when she walked through the hospital doors. She quickly made it to her Honda and jumped inside. Snow was falling lightly and she watched the flakes hit the windshield. She loved snow and everything that went with it. Skiing, snowballs, log fires and the holidays… It was her favorite time of year. And one day she hoped she'd have a family of her own to share it with.

If only she could get the silly and impossible dreams of Brant Parker out of her head.

She popped the key into the ignition, started the car and drove off. The roads were slick, so she took her time getting home. When she pulled up in the driveway it was past five o'clock and she spotted her ginger cat, Boots, sitting idle in the front window. The image made her smile, and she was welcomed by the demanding feline once she'd dusted off her shoes and entered the house.

The place was small and very much in need of a complete renovation. She'd painted the walls in the living area and main bedroom when she'd returned to town for good, but since then she'd been so busy at the hospital, anything else had been put on hold. The kitchen required a complete overhaul as the cupboards were decades old and styled in old-fashioned laminate paneling and bright orange trim. It was retro in the truest sense and not to her taste. But she couldn't really afford to get someone in to do the work until the following summer and wasn't skilled enough to tackle anything more than painting herself. So, it would have to wait.

She dropped her bag, fed the cat and quickly checked her email before she headed to the shower. Within half an hour she was dressed in her favorite long denim skirt, emerald green shirt and mid-heeled boots. She pulled her hair from its ponytail, applied a little makeup and grabbed a small handbag for her wallet and cell phone. She texted Kayla as she was leaving, grabbed her coat and headed outside. She dusted the thin layer of snow off the windshield before she got into her car. The vehicle took a few turns of the key to start, but she was soon on her way.

The O'Sullivan pub was in the center of town and possessed a kind of richly authentic Irish flavor. It was actually a hotel, with fifteen luxurious rooms, two restaurants, a bar, an outdoor garden for private functions and several conference rooms available for rent. The O'Sullivan family was rich and well-known. Although the old man, John O'Sullivan, had retired and his eldest son, Liam, now ran the place, he still walked around with his chest puffed out like he ruled the town and everyone in it. No one crossed the O'Sullivans. No one would dare. The hotel was one of the main draws in the town and that had a lot of pull with the mayor's office. Tourists came to see the old mines, the occasional rodeos, the horse and cattle ranches, and many used the town as a stopover before they crossed the state line. Since the O'Sullivan's hotel was the poshest place to stay, few people objected to paying for their amenities.

She did wonder if that's why Brant had bought the Loose Moose—as a way of sticking it to the O'Sullivans. There was certainly no love lost between the two families. Brant's older brother, Grady, had been married to Liz O'Sullivan, and Lucy knew her parents had never thought a rancher was good enough for their beloved daughter. When Liz died a few years ago things had gotten worse and, according to Colleen Parker, the feud between the two families was now quite intense.

It was early, so she found a spot outside the hotel and parked. She got out, grabbed her coat from the backseat and tossed it over her arm. A few people milled around the front of the hotel, and she recognized a couple of nurses from the hospital and waved as she made her way through the wide doors.

Kayla, Brooke and Ash were already seated at a booth in the bar when she arrived, with a pitcher of sangria between them. The O'Sullivan pub certainly wasn't the average run-of-the-mill kind of drinking establishment. If you wanted beer and a game of pool you went to one of the other cowboy bars in town like Rusty's or the Black Bull. She slid into the booth and raised a brow at the quarter-empty pitcher on the table. "You started without me?"

Brooke tossed her straight blond hair a little and grinned. "You're late. So, of course."

Blue-eyed Ash, whose bobbed hair was the color of copper, smiled and nodded. "I'm off duty."

"And being a museum curator is thirsty work," Kayla said and laughed. "Although I'll be stopping at one drink. But we got you a glass."

Lucy chuckled and stared at her friend, who was easily the most beautiful woman she'd ever known. Kayla's long blond hair and dark brown eyes stopped most men in their tracks.

She lifted the half-filled glass and took a small sip. “Thanks. Are we staying for dinner?”

“Not me,” Brooke said. “I have a foal due within days and with this weather coming in…” She sighed and grinned. “You know how it is.”

Yes, they all knew Brooke lived and breathed for her horses.

“Nor me. I only have a sitter until seven thirty,” Ash replied and inclined a thumb toward Kayla. “And this one has a date.”

Lucy’s gaze widened. “Really? With whom?”

Kayla laughed again. “Assignments. Marking papers for the online class I’m teaching through the community college.”

“Gosh, we’re a boring group,” Lucy said and smiled. “Just as well I have a cat to get home to.”

“You could always ask Hot Stuff over there to take you to dinner,” Kayla suggested and laughed again.

Lucy’s eyes popped wide. *Hot Stuff?* There was no mistaking who she meant. Her friend had been calling Brant that name for years, ever since Lucy had admitted she was crushing on him when she was a teenager.

“He’s here?”

“Yep,” Kayla replied. “Over by the bar, talking to Liam O’Sullivan.”

Lucy looked toward Ash for confirmation. “She’s right. He was here when we arrived. Looks like he’s not too happy about it, either. I don’t think he’s cracked a smile in that time.”

Nothing unusual about that, Lucy thought. She itched to turn around and see for herself, but didn’t want to appear obvious. But she was curious as to why he was with Liam O'Sullivan, considering the family history.

"You know, he's not a complete killjoy," Brooke said about her cousin and gave a little grin. "And if you like, I could ask him for you?"

Lucy almost spat out her sangria. "Don't you dare," she warned. "You know how I feel about—"

"Yes," Brooke assured her and chuckled. "We've known how you feel about him for well over a decade."

God, how foolish that sounded. And, if she were being completely honest with herself, a little pathetic. She certainly didn't want friends thinking she was still *pining* for Brant Parker after so many years. "Well, I *won't* be asking him to take me to dinner," Lucy assured them.

"Pity," Kayla said and chuckled. "Because he hasn't taken his eyes off you since you've been here."

Lucy's cheeks heated. So, he watched her. It didn't mean *anything*. She might be unkissed, untouched and naive, but she was savvy enough to know when a man *wasn't* interested. Even though there were times…well, *occasionally* she had thought that she'd seen interest in his blue eyes. But mostly she thought it simply *wishful thinking* and then got on with knowing he'd never look at her in that way.

She turned her head a little and spotted him. Handsome as ever, he was talking to Liam and she experienced the usual flutter in her belly. His dark hair, strong jaw and blue eyes never failed to affect her on a kind of primal level.

"You're imagining things," she said dismissively and poured another quarter of a glass of sangria to keep her hands busy.

"I know what I saw," Kayla said, still smiling. "I wonder what he's doing talking with Liam."

"I'm sure you'll find out," Lucy said with a grin.

Kayla sighed heavily. "For the last time, I am *not* interested in Liam O'Sullivan."

Ash and Brooke both laughed. "Sure you aren't," Ash said.

"We're just working together on the gallery extension plans, that's all," Kayla insisted.

Lucy was pretty sure there was more to it, but didn't press the issue. She was more interested in knowing why Brant was consorting with his brother's mortal enemy. But since neither things were any of her business, she concentrated on the cocktails and enjoying her friend's company.

Except, Brooke didn't drop the topic. "At least he hasn't wrecked his bike again."

"Not for a couple of months," Lucy said and frowned. "He was lucky he wasn't seriously injured," she added with quiet emphasis.

His last visit to the ER was his third in seven months and had landed him with a dislocated shoulder and cuts and scrapes. The first was another flip from his motorbike. The second was when he'd climbed Kegg's Mountain and taken a tumble that also could have killed him. Why he'd risk his life so carelessly after surviving three tours of the Middle East, Lucy had no idea.

"I guess he's just adventurous," Brooke said, and Lucy saw a shadow of concern in her friend's expression. This was Brant's cousin. Family. Brooke knew him. And clearly she was worried.

"Maybe," Lucy replied and smiled fractionally, eager to change the subject.

Ash bailed at seven fifteen to get home to her eleven-year-old son, Jaye. Lucy hung out with Kayla and Brooke for another ten minutes before they all grabbed their bags and headed out. Brant had left half an hour earlier, without looking at her, without even acknowledging her presence. Kayla managed a vague wave to Liam O'Sullivan before they walked through the doors and into the cold night air.

Lucy grabbed her coat and flipped it over her shoulders. "It's still snowing. Weird for this time of year. Remind me again why I didn't accept the offer to join the hospital in San Francisco?"

"Because you don't like California," Kayla said, shivering. "And you said you'd miss us and this town too much."

"True," Lucy said and grinned. "I'll talk to you both over the weekend."

They hugged goodbye and headed in opposite directions. People were still coming into the hotel and the street out front was getting busy, so she took some time to maneuver her car from its space and drive off.

The main street of Cedar River was typical of countless others in small towns: a mix of old and new buildings, cedar and stucco, some tenanted, some not. There were two sets of traffic lights and one main intersection. Take a left and the road headed toward Rapid City. Go right and there was Nebraska. Over three and a half thousand people called Cedar River home. It sat peacefully in the shadow of the Black Hills and was as picturesque as a scene from a postcard. She loved the town and never imagined living anywhere else. Even while she was away at college, medical school and working at the hospital in Sioux Falls for three years, her heart had always called her home.

Up until recently the town had been two towns—Cedar Creek and Riverbend—separated by a narrow river and a bridge. But after years of negotiating, the townships had formed one larger town called Cedar River. Lucy had supported the merger… It meant more funding for the hospital and the promise of a unified, economically sound community.

Lucy was just about to flick on the radio for the chance to hear the weather report when her car spluttered and slowed, quickly easing to little more than a roll. She steered left and pulled to the curb as the engine coughed and died.

Great…

A few cars passed, all clearly intent on getting home before the snow worsened. Lucy grabbed her bag and pulled out her cell. She could call her automobile club for assistance, but that meant she'd be dragging mechanic Joss Culhane out to give her a tow home. And Joss was a single dad with two little girls to look after and had better things to do than come to her rescue because she'd forgotten about the battery light that had been flashing intermittently all week.

Better she didn't. She was just about to call Kayla to come and get her when she spotted something attached to one of the old buildings flapping in the breeze. A shingle. Recognition coursed through her.

The Loose Moose. Brant's place.

A light shone through one of the front windows. He was home. She knew he lived in the apartment above the tavern. Of course she'd never been up there. But Colleen Parker had told her how he was renovating the tavern while residing in the upstairs rooms.

Lucy got out of the car and wrapped herself in her red woolen coat. Surely, Brant would help her, given the circumstances?

She grabbed her bag and locked the car before she headed toward the old tavern. The old adobe front was boarded up, apart from the two windows, and the heavy double doors were still blackened in spots from the damage caused by the fire eight months before.

Lucy knocked once and waited. She could hear music coming from inside and discreetly peered through one of the windows. There were trestle tables scattered with power tools and neat stacks of timber on the floor near the long bar, and the wall between the remaining booth seats and the back room that had once housed pool tables had been pulled down. She knocked again, louder this time, and then again. The music stopped. By the time the door swung back she was shivering with cold, her knuckles were pink and her patience a little frayed.

Until she saw him. Then her mouth turned dry and her knees knocked for an altogether different reason.

He wore jeans and a navy sweater that molded to his shoulders and chest like a second skin. His dark hair was ruffled, as though he'd just run a hand through it, and the very idea made her palms tingle. His blue eyes shimmered and his jaw was set tightly. He looked surprised to see her on his doorstep. And not one bit welcoming.

But, dear heaven, he is gorgeous.

She forced some words out. "Um, hi."

"Dr. Monero," he said, frowning. "It's a little late for a house call, don't you think?"

She swallowed hard, suddenly nervous. There was no welcome in his words. She jutted her chin. "Oh, call me Lucy," she insisted and then waved a backward hand. "My car has stopped just outside. I think it's the battery. And I didn't want to call for a tow because my mechanic has two little kids and I thought it was too much to ask for him to come out in this weather and I was wondering if… I thought you might…"

"You thought I might what?"

Lucy wanted to turn and run. But she stayed where she was and took a deep breath. "I thought you might be able to help. Or give me a lift home."

His brows shot up. "You did?"

She shrugged. "Well, I know it's only a few blocks away, but the paths are slippery and the snow doesn't seem to be easing anytime soon."

His gaze flicked upward for a second toward the falling snow and then to her car. "Give me your keys," he instructed and held out his hand.

Lucy dropped the keys into his palm and watched as he strode past her and to her car. He was in the car and had the hood up in seconds. Lucy tucked her coat collar around her neck and joined him by the vehicle. He closed the driver's door and moved around the front, bending over the engine block. Lucy watched, captivated and suddenly breathless over the sheer masculine image he evoked. There was something elementally attractive about him…something heady and fascinating. Being around him felt as decadent as being behind the counter in a candy store. He had a narcotic power that physically affected her from the roots of her hair to the soles of her feet. And she'd never responded to a man in that way before.

Not even close.

Sure, she'd crushed on several of the O'Sullivan or Culhane brothers back in high school. But Brant Parker had never been far from her thoughts. Returning to Cedar River had only amplified the feeling over the years. Being around him made her realize how real that attraction still was. She liked him. She wanted him. It was that simple. It was that complicated.

"Battery's dead," he said, closing the hood.

Lucy smiled. "Well, at least that means I remembered to put gas in the tank."

He didn't respond. He simply looked at her. Deeply. Intently. As if, in that moment, there was nothing else. No one else. Just the two of them, standing in the evening snow, with the streetlight casting shadows across the sidewalk.

"I'll take you home," he said and walked back toward the Loose Moose.

Lucy followed and stood by the doors. "I'll wait here if you like."

Brant turned and frowned. "I have to get my jacket and keys, and my truck is parked out back. So you might as well come inside."

He didn't sound like he wanted her in his home. In fact, he sounded like it was the last thing he wanted. But, undeterred, she followed him across the threshold and waited as he shut the door.

"You've been busy," she said as she walked through the room and dropped her bag on the bar. "The renovations are coming along."

"That was the idea when I bought the place."

Lucy turned and stared at him. He really was a disagreeable ass. She wondered for the thousandth time why she wasted her energy being attracted to him when he made no effort to even be nice to her.

Not one to back down, she propped her hands on her hips. "You know, I was wondering something… Is it simply me you dislike or people in general?"

His jaw tightened. Hallelujah. Connection. Something to convince her he wasn't a cold fish incapable of response. His gaze was unwavering, blistering and so intense she could barely take a breath.

"I don't dislike you, Dr. Monero."

She shook her head. “My case in point. I’ve asked you half a dozen times to call me Lucy. The very fact you don’t speaks louder than words. I know you *can* be nice because I’ve seen you with your mom and brother and nieces. At least when we were kids you were mostly civil…but now all I get from you is—”

“You talk too much.”

Lucy was silenced immediately. She looked at him and a heavy heat swirled between them. She wasn’t imagining it. It was there…real and palpable. And mutual. As inexperienced as she was, Lucy recognized the awareness that suddenly throbbed between them.

Attraction. Chemistry. Sex.

All of the above. All very mutual.

And she had no real clue what to do about it.

Chapter Two

Lucy Monero was a walking, talking temptation. And Brant wanted her. It took all of his willpower to *not* take her in his arms and kiss her like crazy.

But he stayed where he was, watching her, noticing how her hair shone from the light beaming from above. Her dazzling green eyes were vivid and suggestive, but also filled with a kind of uncertainty that quickly captivated him. Lucy had a way of stopping him in his tracks with only a look. So he didn't dare touch her. Didn't dare kiss her. Didn't dare talk to her, even though there were times when he thought he'd like nothing else than to listen to her voice or to hear her breathless laughter.

When they were kids she'd hung around the ranch, often watching him and his brother break and train the horses from the sidelines, her head always tucked into a book. She'd been quiet and reserved back then, not trying to grow up before her time by wearing makeup or trendy clothes. When her dad died, her mom had sold the small ranch and they'd moved into town, so he hadn't seen her as much. His own dad had died around that time, too, and with twenty-year-old Grady taking over the reins at their family ranch and Brant deciding on a military career midway through senior year, there wasn't any time to spend thinking about the shy, studious girl who never seemed to be able to meet his gaze.

Not so now, he thought. She'd grown up and gained a kind of mesmerizing poise along the way. Oh, she'd always been pretty—but now she was beautiful and tempting and had firmly set her sights on what she wanted.

Which appeared to be him.

Brant wasn't egotistical. But he recognized the look in her eyes every time they met. And he wasn't about to get drawn into *anything* with Lucy Monero. She was pure hometown. A nice girl who wanted romance, a wedding and a white picket fence. He'd heard enough about it and her virtues from his mom and Brooke. Well, it wasn't for him. He didn't do romance. And he wasn't about to get involved with a woman who had marriage on her mind.

"You're staring at me."

Her words got his thoughts on track and Brant felt heat quickly creep up his back and neck. His jaw clenched and he straightened his shoulders. "So, I'll just get my jacket and take you home."

"Is everything okay?" she asked quietly.

"What?"

She tilted her head a little and regarded him with her usual intensity. "You seem…tense."

It irritated him to no end that she could see through him like that. "I'm fine," he lied.

Her brows came up. "I'm pretty sure you're not."

"Is there a point you're trying to make?"

She shrugged one shoulder. "You know, most times we meet, you barely acknowledge me. At first I thought it was because you were just settling back in to civilian life and that small talk was really not your thing. But then I've seen you with your family and you seem relaxed and friendly enough around them. And you were with Liam O'Sullivan earlier and didn't end up punching him in the face, so that interaction must have turned out okay. So maybe it's just me."

Brant ignored the way his heart thundered behind his ribs. *It is you.* He wasn't about to get drawn into her little world. Not now. Not ever. He had too much going on. Too much baggage banging around in his head. Too many memories that could unglue him if he let someone in.

"Like I said, you talk too much."

She laughed, the sound wispy and sort of throaty and so damned sexy it sucked the air from his lungs. He was tempted to take the three steps he needed to be beside her. Maybe kissing her would get her out of his system. Maybe it was exactly the thing he needed to keep her out of his thoughts. But he stayed where he was, both irritated and fascinated by the relentless effect she had on him without even trying. And he knew the only way around it was to stay out of her way. To avoid her. To ignore her. To keep himself separate, as he had for the past eight months, and not get drawn into the land of the living where he would be forced to take part. Instead he'd stay on the sidelines, pretending everything was fine. Pretending *he* was fine. So his mom and brother didn't work out that he was now a shadow of the man he'd once been.

"So, I'm right. It *is* just me?" she asked, stepping a little closer. "Why? Are you worried that I might work out that underneath all your brooding indifference there's actually a decent sort of man?"

"Not at all," he replied quietly. "*Dr. Monero*, the truth is I don't think about you from one moment to the next."

It was a mean thing to say. He knew. She knew it. And he hated the way the words tasted in his mouth. He wasn't cruel. He wasn't good at it. He felt clumsy even saying the words. But he had to try to keep her at a distance.

"I see." Her eyes shadowed over for a second. She looked…hurt. Wounded. And the notion cut through him like a knife. He didn't want to hurt her. He didn't want to have any feelings when it came to Lucy Monero. "Okay. Fine. You've made yourself perfectly clear. Now, I think I'll find my own way home."

She was past him and by the door in seconds. As she rattled the doorknob, Brant took a few strides and reached her, placing a hand on either side of the jamb. She turned and gasped, looking up, so close he could feel her breath on his chin.

"Lucy..."

The sound of her name on his lips reverberated through him, sending his heart hammering and his blood surging through his veins. She was trapped, but didn't move, didn't do anything but hold his gaze steady. And this, he thought as he stared down into her face, was exactly why he needed to keep his distance. There was heat between them…heat generated by a sizzling attraction that had the power to knock him off his feet.

"Don't…please…" she said shakily, her bottom lip trembling fractionally.

Brant stepped back and dropped his arms instantly. "I'm not going to hurt you."

She nodded. "I know that. I didn't mean I thought you would. It's just that…being around you…it's confusing."

She was right about that!

"It's like you ignore me as though I don't exist," she

went on to say. "But sometimes you look at me as if… as if…"

"As if what?" he shot back.

"As if you do…like me."

"Of course I do," he admitted raggedly, taking a breath, hoping she couldn't see how messed up he was. "But I'm not in the market for anything serious. Not with you."

There…it was out in the open. Now she could move on and stop looking at him as though he could give her all she wanted. Because he couldn't. He didn't have it in him. Not now. He'd been through too much. Seen too much. He wasn't good company. He wasn't boyfriend or husband material. He was better off alone.

"Why not?" she asked.

Nothing...

Brant sighed heavily. "I'd prefer not to get into it."

"Oh, no," she said and crossed her arms, pushing her chest up, which instantly grabbed his attention.

God, her curves were mesmerizing. He looked to the floor for a moment to regather his good sense and hoped she'd stop talking. But no such luck.

"You don't get to make a bold statement like that and then think you're off the hook. What's wrong with me?" Her brows rose again. "I'm honest, intelligent, loyal and respectable, and have good manners. I even have all my own teeth."

Brant laughed loudly. God, it felt good to laugh. There was something so earnest about Lucy it was impossible to remain unaffected by her. During the past few weeks he'd often heard her soft laughter through the corridors of the veterans home and wondered how it would feel to be on the receiving end of such a sweet, sincere sound. And he wanted to hear it again.

"Well, I guess if I was buying a pony, all bases would be covered."

Her chuckle started out soft and then morphed into a full-on, loud guffaw. By the time she was done there were tears on her cheeks. She wiped them away and thrust out her chin.

"Wow…you do have a sense of humor." Her eyes shimmered. "Your cousin was right, you're not always a complete killjoy."

"No," he said easily. "Not always."

"So, this being a jerk thing…that's something you save especially for me?"

Brant's mouth twitched. "I have to get my keys," he said, ignoring the question. "Wait here."

Her eyes sparkled. "Aren't you going to invite me upstairs?"

To his apartment? His bedroom? "Not a chance," he said and strode off without looking back.

Lucy wrapped her arms around herself and wandered through the tavern. Every sense she possessed was on red alert. By the door he'd been so close…close enough that she could have taken a tiny step and been pressed against him. The heat from his skin had scorched hers. The warmth of his breath had made her lips tingle with anticipation. It was desire unlike any she'd known before. And she wanted it. She wanted him. She wanted his kiss, his touch. She wanted every part of him to cover every part of her.

And she shook all over, thinking about her false bravado. She'd never spoken to man in such a blatantly flirtatious tone before. But being around Brant was unlike anything she'd ever experienced. As *inexperienced* as she was, flirting and verbally sparring with him seemed to have a will and a power all of its own.

"Ready?"

He was back, standing by the steps that led upstairs. Lucy swallowed hard and nodded. "Sure. Thanks."

He shrugged loosely. "My truck's out back."

"No motorbike?"

He raised a brow and began to walk toward the rear of the building. "Not in this weather."

He was right, but the idea of being behind him on his motorbike, holding on to him, being so close she'd be able to feel his heartbeat, made her pulse race.

"So you're only reckless with yourself. That's good to know."

Brant stopped midstride and turned. "What?"

Lucy held out three fingers. "That's how many times you've been in hospital in the past seven months. Twice off your bike because you were speeding and once when you thought it was a good idea to climb Kegg's Mountain—alone—and without the proper gear, I might add."

"You're still talking too much," he muttered and then kept walking.

Lucy followed him down the long hallway, past the kitchen and restrooms, and then through the rear door. He waited for her to walk outside and locked the door. It was still snowing lightly and she took quick steps toward the beat-up, blue Ford pickup parked outside. He opened the passenger door, ushered her inside, strode around the front of the vehicle and slid into the driver's seat.

"What's your address?" he asked.

Lucy gave him directions and dropped her bag into her lap.

She expected him to immediately start the truck and drive off. But he didn't. He put the key in the ignition but placed both hands on the steering wheel. And then he spoke.

"I wasn't speeding. My bike blew a tire the first time and the second time I swerved to avoid hitting a dog that was on the road."

It was meant to put her in her place. To shut her up. To end the conversation.

But Lucy wasn't one to be silenced. "And the mountain?"

"I was unprepared. Not a mistake I would make again." He started the engine and thrust the gear into Reverse. "Satisfied?"

Lucy's skin tingled. The idea of being satisfied by Brant Parker had her insides doing flip-flops. Of course, he wasn't being suggestive, but Lucy couldn't help thinking how good a lover he would be. Not that she would have anything to make a comparison with. But she had a vivid imagination and she had certainly fantasized about being between the sheets with the man beside her.

She smiled sweetly. "I guess I didn't hear the whole story because I didn't attend to you the night you were brought into the ER."

He shifted gears again and turned into the street. "I thought my mother would have kept you updated. You and she seem to have become quite the twosome."

"I like your mom," Lucy replied. "She's a good friend."

"Yeah, my mom is a good person." He turned left. "She also likes to play matchmaker."

Lucy's mouth twitched. She knew that. Colleen had been gently pushing her in Brant's direction for months. "Does that make you nervous?" she asked, turning her gaze. "I mean, now she's got Grady settled and engaged to Marissa, do you think you're next?"

She watched his profile. Impassive. Unmoving. Like a

rock. But he was trying too hard. The pulse in his cheek was beating madly. He wasn't so unmoved. He was simply reining his feelings in…as usual.

"She's wasting her time."

Lucy tried not to be offended and managed a brittle laugh. "Considering how happy your brother is now, you can't blame your mom for wanting the same for you."

"I'm not my brother."

No, he wasn't. She knew Grady Parker. Oh, he still had the Parker pride and was a teeny bit arrogant, but he was a good-natured, hardworking family man with three little girls to raise and had recently found love again with Marissa Ellis. The wedding was only a couple of weeks away and Lucy knew Brant was standing as his brother's best man. She'd been invited, more to please Colleen Parker than anything else, she was sure. And since Brooke and Ash were both going and she liked Marissa and Grady, she was delighted to be part of their special day.

"Have you got a speech prepared?" Lucy asked, shifting the subject. "For the wedding, I mean. I hear you're the best man. That should be a fun gig…even for you."

He pulled the truck up outside her house, set the vehicle into Park and switched off the ignition. Then he turned in his seat and looked at her, his jaw set rigid. Boy, he was tense. And the intensity of it crackled the air between them. Lucy met his gaze and held it. Felt the heat of his stare as though he was touching her, stroking her, caressing her. She shuddered and she knew he was aware of the effect he had over her. A tiny smile tugged at the corner of his mouth, as though he knew he shouldn't react but couldn't resist.

If he moved, if he so much as lowered his defenses in any way, Lucy would have planted herself against him and begged for his kiss. She wanted it. Longed for it. But he continued to look at her, into her, making her achingly aware of the intimacy of the small space they shared.

"Even for me?" he intoned, his deep voice as intense as a caress. "I do know how to have a good time, despite what you think."

Lucy's bravado spiked. "Really?"

He inhaled heavily. "What is it you want, Dr. Monero?"

The million-dollar question. Bravado was fine when it wasn't challenged. But under scrutiny, Lucy quickly became unsettled. "I'm not… I don't…"

"You want something. Is it me?" he asked bluntly. "Is that what you want?"

Color smacked her cheeks. "I just want—"

"Why?" he asked, cutting her off. "Why me? You could have anyone you—"

"Chemistry," she said quickly, dying inside. "Attraction."

"Sex?"

Lucy stilled. She didn't want to think her reaction to him was merely physical. But since she did find him more attractive than she'd ever found any other man, perhaps she was blinded by those feelings? Maybe her daydreams about getting to know him, being around him and spending time with him were exactly that. Dreams. And foolish remnants of an old teenaged infatuation. She'd spent college and medical school wrapped in a bubble—wary of involvement with anyone because of what had happened to her roommate. But once she was back in Cedar River—more confident and older and able to meet his gaze head-on—Lucy had believed she would somehow be able to capture his attention.

But that hadn't happened. He'd ignored her. Despite her smiles and friendly attention.

And the more he ignored her, the more she wanted

him. His indifference became fuel for her teenaged fantasies and starved libido. So maybe it was just sex and she was simply too inexperienced to recognize it for what it was.

"What's wrong with that, anyway?" she shot back as heat climbed over her skin.

His gaze narrowed. "What's wrong with sex? Nothing… if that's all you're after." He reached out and touched her hair, trapped a few strands between his fingertips. It was the first time he'd touched her and it was electric. "But you don't strike me as the casual-sex kind of girl, Doc Monero. In fact, I'd bet my boots you are the white-picket-fence, happy-ever-after kind."

God, if he only knew, he'd probably run a mile.

"That's quite a judgment. And what are you? Only casual, no happy-ever-after?"

"Close enough," he said and returned his hands to the wheel.

"Back at the tavern you said you…liked me…so which is it?"

"Neither. Both. You're wasting your time with me. I'm not marriage material. So, good night."

Humiliation coursed through her veins and Lucy grabbed her bag and placed it in her lap. She got the message loud and clear. He was awful. Just awful. She swallowed the lump in her throat. "Are you going to walk me to my door?"

"This isn't a date," he said quietly.

He was such a jerk, and he was right about one thing: she was seriously wasting her time being attracted to him. Lucy set her teeth together and opened the door. "Thanks for the lift. I'll get my car towed in the morning. Good night."

"Good night…Lucy."

She got out, shut the door and stomped up the path and to the front door. While she was opening the door she realized he was still parked by the curb. So maybe he did have some chivalry in him. Ha—but not enough. As she got inside and peeked through the lace curtains to watch him finally drive away, Lucy decided she was going to forget all about him and spend her nights dreaming of someone else. Anyone else.

And the sooner she started the better.

Brant had been visiting his mother's home for lunch nearly every Saturday since he'd returned from his last tour. Colleen insisted they have a family catch-up and he didn't mind. He loved his mom, even though she drove him nuts with her attempts to interfere in his personal life. He knew there were only good intentions in her meddling, so he usually laughed it off and ignored her. But today—the morning after the whole Lucy-Monero-and-her-broken-down-car thing—Colleen was onto him the moment he stepped foot into her kitchen.

"I went into town early to get eggs and milk and saw Lucy's car outside the tavern," she said, her wide-eyed gaze all speculation and curiosity.

Brant walked around the timber countertop, grabbed a mug from the cupboard and poured coffee. "Her car broke down. I gave her a lift home."

And acted like a total horse's ass.

"She didn't spend the night?"

Color crept up his neck. His mother looked disappointed. Boy, sometimes he wished he had one of those parents who didn't want to talk about every single thing. "No, Mom, she didn't."

Colleen smiled. "You know, it wouldn't hurt you to encourage her a little. She's a nice girl. Smart. Pretty.

Sweet. And she has a kind spirit. I think she'd be a good match for you."

Brant sighed. "Are we really going to do this every Saturday?"

She grinned. "Every Saturday? I don't think I mentioned it last weekend."

"Oh, yeah, you did." Brant sugared his coffee and sat at the table. "I'm not in the market for a relationship right now," he said for the umpteenth time. "I need time to—"

"I know that's what you think," she said gently, cutting him off. "But I'm concerned about you."

"I know you're worried about me, Mom, but I'm okay," he assured her.

"You went through a lot over there," she said, her eyes glittering. "More than any of us will probably ever know. You're my son and I'm always going to be looking out for you, regardless of how old you are. When you have a child of your own you will understand what I mean."

"She's right, you know."

They both looked toward the doorway. His brother, Grady, stood on the threshold.

Brant frowned as his brother came into the room and sat. "You said you wouldn't encourage her," Brant reminded him.

Grady shrugged. "When she's right, she's right. I don't think it would matter how old my girls are, I'll always be on hand to make sure they're all right."

"See," Colleen said and smiled. "At least one of my sons had the good sense to listen to me."

Brant groaned. "Just because you meddled in his life and got him on the way to the altar, don't think you are going to do that with me. I have no intention of getting married anytime soon."

"You're thirty years old," his mom reminded him quietly. "And a civilian. You can have a normal life now, Brant."

No, he couldn't…

But he wasn't about to go down that road with his mother and brother. They didn't know much about what had happened before he'd left Afghanistan for good. He hardly dared think about it, let alone consider sharing it with his family. If they knew, they'd close ranks, smother him, give him sympathy and understanding when he deserved neither. In his mind, despite how hard he tried to get the thought out of his head, he was still a soldier. Still standing on the ridge. Still hearing the gunfire and the screams of the men in his unit who'd lost their lives that day.

"So where are the girls this morning?" he asked his brother, shifting the subject.

"With Marissa, getting their hair done." Grady grinned. "It's a practice run for their wedding-day hair."

Brant admired his brother. He'd raised his three young daughters alone since his wife, Liz, had died a couple of years earlier. Brant admired Marissa, too. His soon-to-be sister-in-law adored his nieces and had effortlessly stepped into her role as stepmother to the girls since she'd accepted his brother's proposal. Grady was a good man. The best he knew. And Brant was pleased his brother had found happiness again.

"O'Sullivan increased the offer," Brant said and drank some coffee.

Grady tapped his fist on the table. "Son of a bitch!"

"I didn't accept," he said when he saw his brother's swiftly gathering rage. "And I won't."

"Liam O'Sullivan believes he can have and do whatever he wants, just like his old man," Grady said and scowled. "The whole bunch of them think they're so damned entitled. No wonder Liz couldn't wait to get away from them. He only wants the Loose Moose because he doesn't want the competition. I heard he's been sniffing around Rusty's again, too. When Ted Graham finally does decide he wants to retire, O'Sullivan will be circling like a hyena."

"I told Ted I'd be interested in Rusty's if it comes on the market. He's not foolish enough to let the O'Sullivans get hold of the place. He hates them as much as you do."

Grady grunted. "You want two pubs? That's ambitious."

Brant shrugged. "Gotta make a living doing something."

"I thought you might want to come back to the ranch where you belong."

"I'm not much of a cowboy these days," he said, grinning.

"You're good with horses," Grady said generously. "Would be a shame to waste that skill entirely."

"You know I'll always give you a hand if you need it. But not full-time."

Grady nodded. "What about school?" his brother queried. "You said you were thinking of studying business at the community college."

"I still might."

"You could teach French at the night school, too," Grady suggested.

"I could," Brant replied, thinking about his options. "If I wasn't so busy with the Loose Moose."

"How are the renovations coming?"

"Slow," he said. "But I knew it would take a while. Doing the majority of it myself saves dollars but takes more time."

"If you need money to—"

"It's fine." Brant waved a hand. "I don't need your money."

"It's family money," Grady corrected. "The ranch is just as much yours as mine. And I would consider the tavern an investment. Dad and Uncle Joe and Granddad used to love the old place, remember?"

He did remember. It was one of the reasons why he'd been so keen to buy the tavern. "I'll let you know," he said, trying to fob his brother off as gently as he could.

Grady had a good heart but still acted as though he had to shoulder the brunt of all family issues. It was an "older brother thing," he was certain. When Grady had taken over the ranch he'd made it into one of the most successful in the county. Brant admired Grady's determination and commitment to the family, but he needed to do this alone. He needed to forge a life for himself that was of his own making.

"So, about this thing with Lucy Monero?" Grady asked.

"There's nothing going on between us," he assured his brother and looked toward their mother, who was cracking eggs into a bowl at the counter and pretending not to listen. "So, drop it. That means both of you."

"Can't," Colleen said and grinned. "Not when one of my kids is troubled."

Brant looked toward his brother for a little support, but Grady was nodding. Great. Suddenly, Saturday lunch had turned into some kind of intervention. Next, his mom would be suggesting he visit the shrink at the local veterans home.

"I was just talking to Dr. Allenby the other day about…"

Yep, right on schedule, he thought, and pushed his mother's words out of his head as she rattled on. He didn't need a shrink. He'd seen too many of them after Operation Oscar had gone down so badly. Three of his team had lost their lives. It had been two days of hell he wanted to forget. And he would, over time. If only his mom and brother would let up.

"I don't need a shrink."

His mother continued to whisk the eggs. "Then what about talking to someone else. Like me? Or your brother? Or even Lucy?" she suggested. "She's a doctor...and a good one."

Brant expelled an exasperated breath. "Mom, I'm fine. You gotta let this go, okay? I am happy," he lied. "I have you guys and the Loose Moose... For the moment, that's all I have room for. Working on restoring the tavern keeps my head clear, if that makes sense. And it's all the therapy I need."

That was the truth, at least. Sure, he was lonely, but better to be lonely than to bog someone else down with the train wreck his life had become. He probably just needed to get laid. It had been a while. He did the calculation in his head and inwardly grimaced. Man, he seriously needed to get out more. He still had friends in town, but going out with his old high school buddies, drinking beer, playing pool and talking smack didn't really cut it anymore. He wasn't twenty years old. He wasn't blinded by youth or ignorance. He'd seen the world and life at its darkest and would never be able to escape who he had become. Finding someone to share that with seemed impossible. The occasional one-night stand was all he allowed himself. And since Lucy Monero was not a one-night-stand kind of woman, he knew he had to keep avoiding her.

By the time he left his mother's it was nearly two. He headed to the hardware store to pick up a few things and spent the remainder of the afternoon working on the walls in the front part of the tavern. Turning in to bed around ten, he woke up at six on Sunday morning to get an early start, planning to spend the day sanding back the long cedar bar. But at one o'clock he got a call from Grady to say Uncle Joe had been taken to the hospital and was in the emergency room. It took him five minutes to change and head out and another fifteen to get to the hospital. He called Grady again once he was out of the truck and headed for the ER.

By the time he reached Reception he felt as though his chest might explode. The woman behind the counter said she'd inquire after his uncle and told him to wait.

Great. Exactly what he didn't want to do.

He knew Grady was on his way to the hospital, so he paced the room for a few minutes and then finally sat. The hospital sounds reverberated in his eardrums. Phones, beepers, gurneys, heels clicking over tiles. Each sound seemed louder than the last.

He sat for five minutes, swamped by a building helplessness that was suffocating.

When he could stand it no more he got up and headed back to the counter. "Is there any news about my uncle?"

The fifty-something woman scowled a little and flicked through some charts on the desk. "No, nothing yet."

"Then can you find someone who might know something?"

She scowled again and Brant's impatience rose. He wasn't usually a hothead. Most of the time he was calm and in complete control. Twelve years of military training had ingrained those traits into him. But he didn't feel calm now. He felt as though he could barely stand to be in his own skin.

"Brant?"

He knew that voice.

Turning his head, he saw Lucy and relief flooded through him. In some part of his mind he wondered how she had the power to do that, to soothe his turbulent emotions. Just knowing she was there somehow made things easier. Better. He swiveled on his heels and watched as she walked toward him, wearing scrubs and a white coat. Brant met her gaze and swallowed hard.

"You're here."

"I'm here," she said and smiled fractionally. "What do you know?"

"Not much," he said and shook his head. "What happened?"

Her eyes gave it away. It was serious. "He had a heart attack."

A heart attack? Fear coursed through his blood. "Is he…is he dead?"

The second it took for her to answer seemed like an hour. "No."

Brant fought back the emotion clogging his throat. "Is he going to make it?"

She nodded slowly. "I think so."

"Thank God," Brant breathed and, without thinking, reached out and hauled her into his arms.

Chapter Three

Lucy melted.

She'd never pegged Brant as a hugger. Nor did she want to think about what was going on in the minds of the two nurses at the reception desk. Cedar River was a small town. She was a doctor on staff and the most gorgeous man on the planet was holding her so tightly she didn't dare breathe.

There might be talk. Innuendo. But she didn't care. In that moment he needed her. Wanted her. It might be fleeting. It might be the only time she would ever get to feel what it was like to be in his arms. She heard his heart beating and felt the steady thud against her ear. His chest was broad, hard, the perfect place to rest her head, and all her plans to get him out of her mind quickly disappeared.

When he released her she was breathing deeply, conscious of the sudden intimacy between them. He pulled away and dropped his arms, watching her, his gaze so intense it weakened her knees. There was something in his eyes, a kind of wary vulnerability that tugged at her heartstrings.

"Sorry," he said quietly, clearly aware they were being observed by the two women at the desk. "That wasn't appropriate."

Maybe not, she thought, but it sure felt good. It wasn't the first time she been embraced in the waiting room. Relatives of patients had done it before when they had received news, good and bad. But this was different. This was Brant. Lucy forced some movement into her limbs and gathered her composure. She was a doctor and needed to act like one.

"It's fine, don't worry about it. I can take you to see your uncle now."

He nodded. "Thank you."

"We've done a few preliminary tests and it looks as though he has an arterial blockage. So he may need surgery," she explained as she used her key card to open the doors that led to the small emergency room. "We'll keep him here under observation tonight and then he'll be transported to the hospital in Rapid City tomorrow. They have excellent cardiology and surgical departments there and he'll be in really good hands."

He walked beside her through Triage, his expression impassive and unreadable. Lucy linked her hands together and headed for the cubicle at the far end of the room. She eased the curtain back. Joe Parker was resting and she leaned a little closer toward Brant to speak.

"He's asleep. I know his pallor looks a little gray, but that's not unusual after an episode like he's had. We'll let him rest for a while and do his OBS again in half an hour. You can sit with him if you like."

Brant nodded and sat. "Thank you."

Lucy lingered for a moment. “We’ll do our very best for him. He’s a special man and, despite his age, he’s quite strong.”

“Yeah, he is.”

She knew how much the older man meant to Brant. She’d witnessed his affection for Joe Parker many times when he’d come to visit him at the veterans home. And Colleen had told her about the special bond they shared. They were both soldiers. They’d both fought for their country and had seen war and destruction and death. It was easy to understand why Brant cared so much for his uncle and had such a strong connection to him.

“I’ll come back in a little while,” she said and lightly touched Brant’s shoulder. He tensed immediately and she quickly pulled her hand away.

She left the cubicle and pulled the curtains together. There were three other patients in the ER. A woman with a nasty burn on her arm, a toddler with a fever and a teenage boy with a fishing hook through his thumb. She checked on the baby and was pleased that his fever had gone down fractionally, and then instructed one of the triage nurses to get the teenager prepared so she could remove the hook. By the time she was done a little over half an hour had passed and she headed back to Joe Parker’s cubicle.

Grady and Colleen were both there, bending the rules since regulation stated only two visitors were allowed at a time. But Colleen was well-known at the hospital and sometimes rules needed to be broken. Colleen was sitting in the chair and her sons flanked either side of the bed. Joe was awake and smiled broadly when she pulled back the curtain.

“Here she is,” he said. “My guardian angel. She’s been looking after me since I got here.”

Lucy grinned. "Well, you're a model patient, so it's been easy."

"Never a more beautiful girl have I ever seen," Joe said and chuckled. "Makes me wish I was forty years younger."

Lucy smiled at his outrageous flirting and glanced toward Brant. He was watching her with blistering intensity and she quickly shifted her gaze. "How are you feeling?" she asked, grabbing the chart from the foot of the bed.

"Better for seein' you, Doc," he said and winked.

"Joe," Colleen chastised her much older brother-in-law gently. "Behave yourself."

Joe Parker smiled again, wrinkling his cheeks. "Ha! There's no fool like an old fool, right, Doc?"

He made a breathless sound and Lucy stepped toward the bed and grasped his wrist. He was overdoing it. She urged him to lay back and rest. She checked him over and scribbled notes in his chart. When she was done she asked Grady to walk with her outside the cubicle. The eldest Parker son had his uncle's medical power of attorney and she wanted to keep the family updated on his condition.

"It was a mild-range heart attack," she explained once she and Grady were out of earshot. "But I'm concerned enough to send him to Rapid City for a full set of testing. He may need surgery sooner rather than later, but the cardiologist there will make that call. For the moment he is stable and out of pain."

Grady nodded and she was struck by how alike the brothers were. Same color hair, same eyes, same tough jaw. Grady was a little taller than his brother, but Brant was broader through the shoulders. And Grady always looked happy…like he had some great secret to life. Whereas Brant…? Lucy only saw caution and resistance in his gaze. For the moment, though, her only concern was Joe Parker's welfare. She explained the procedure for transporting him to the larger hospital and when she was done asked if he had any questions.

"No," Grady replied. "I do know Brant will want to go with him. They're very close."

She nodded. "I can arrange something." She turned to walk away when Grady said her name. "What is it?"

He shrugged loosely. "About Brant. I know this might not be the right time to say anything…but do you think you could talk to the counselor at the veterans home about perhaps having a word with him…kind of on the down-low, if you know what I mean?"

Lucy's skin prickled. "Do you think he needs counseling?"

"I think when he was a solider he went through some bad stuff and doesn't want to talk about it," Grady said and sighed. "Not even to me or Mom."

Lucy thought that, too. She knew enough about PTSD to recognize the signs. His isolation, irritability and moodiness could definitely be attributed to something like that. Of course, she had no idea what he'd witnessed in service to his country. But if his brother was concerned, that was enough for Lucy to do what she could to help.

"I could have a quiet word with Dr. Allenby. He comes to the home once a week and he's trained to deal with veterans, particularly combat soldiers."

Grady nodded. "Yes, my mom has mentioned him. That's great. I'd really appreciate it if you could do that. But we might want to keep this between us, okay?"

Going behind Brant's back didn't sit well with her conscience. This was a conversation the Parker family needed to have together. But she could clearly see the concern in his brother's eyes and that was enough to get her agreement for the moment. "Don't think there'll be a problem with that. Your brother hardly talks to me."

"Self-preservation," Grady said and grinned.

"What?"

His grin widened. "You know how guys are. We always do things stupid-ass backward. Ask Marissa how much I screwed up in the beginning. Ignoring her was all I could do to keep from going crazy."

Lucy's mouth creased into a smile. "You know he'd hate the fact we're out here talking about him, don't you?"

"Yep," Grady replied. "Just as well we're on the same side."

Lucy's smiled deepened. "I'll see what I can do."

Grady returned to his uncle's bedside and Lucy headed to the cafeteria for a break. She ordered tea and a cranberry muffin and sat by the window, looking out toward the garden, an unread magazine open on the table in front of her. The place was empty except for the two people behind the counter and a couple of orderlies who were chatting over coffee in the far corner. She liked days like this. Quiet days. It gave her time to think. The hospital was small but catered to a wide area and some days she didn't have time for breaks.

"Can I talk to you?"

Lucy looked up from her tea. Brant stood beside the small table. "Oh…sure."

He pulled out the chair opposite. "Can I get you anything? More coffee?"

"Tea," she corrected and shook her head. "And I'm good. What can I do for you?"

It sounded so perfunctory…when inside she was churning. He looked so good in jeans and a black shirt and leather jacket. His brown hair was long, too, as it had been in high school, curling over his collar a little—a big change from the regulation military crew cut she was used to seeing when he came back to town in between tours. There was a small scar on his left temple and another under his chin, and she wondered how he'd gotten them. War wounds? Perhaps they were old football injuries or from school-yard antics? Or when he used to work horses with his brother? He'd always looked good in the saddle. She had spent hours pretending to have her nose in a book while she'd watched him ride from the sidelines. At twelve she'd had stars in her eyes. At twenty-seven she felt almost as foolish.

She took a breath and stared at him. "So…what is it?"

"My uncle is seventy-three years old, and I know he has health issues and might not have a lot of time left. I also know that he trusts you."

"And?" she prompted.

He shrugged one shoulder. "And I was thinking that once he gets to the hospital in Rapid City there will be a whole lot of people there who he doesn't trust poking and prodding and making judgment calls and decisions about him."

Lucy stilled. "And?" she prompted again.

"And he'd probably prefer it if you were around to see to things."

She eyed him shrewdly. "*He* would?"

His other shoulder moved. "Okay… *I* would."

"You want me to go to the hospital with him?"

"Well…yes."

"I'm not on staff there," she explained, increasingly conscious of his intense gaze. "I couldn't interfere with his treatment or be part of his appointments with specialists."

"I know that," Brant replied softly, his attention unwavering. "But you could be there to explain things… you know, to make sense of things."

Lucy drank some tea and then placed the paper cup on the table. "With you?"

He shrugged again. "Sure."

"Won't that go against your determination to avoid me and my wicked plans to ensnare you with my white picket fence?"

His eyes darkened. She was teasing him. And Brant Parker clearly didn't like to be teased.

"This is about my uncle," he replied, his jaw clenching. "Not us."

The silly romantic in her wanted to swoon at the way he said the word *us*. But she didn't.

"I do have the day off tomorrow," she said, thinking she was asking for a whole lot of complications by agreeing to his request. But she did genuinely care about Joe Parker.

"So…yes?" he asked.

Lucy nodded slowly. "Sure. I'll arrange for the ambulance to leave here around nine in the morning and we can follow in my car."

"I'll drive. We'll take my truck."

Lucy gave in to the laughter she felt. "Boy, you're predictable. Clearly my little Honda isn't macho enough."

"I need to get some building supplies from Rapid City," he shot back, unmoving. "I don't think the footrest for the bar that I'm having made will fit in your *little Honda*, Dr. Monero. Besides the fact that your car is unreliable."

"I had my car towed and the battery replaced yesterday, so it's as good as new." Her cheeks colored. "And I thought we agreed you were going to call me Lucy?"

A smile tugged at the corner of his mouth. "Did we? Okay, *Lucy*, I'll pick you up around nine."

His uncle looked much better the following day, but Brant was still pleased he was going to be assessed in Rapid City. He was also pleased that Lucy Monero had agreed to go with him. He knew it was a big favor to ask. But she'd agreed, even when she had every reason not to. He'd acted like a stupid jerk the night she'd broken down outside the tavern.

He waited in the foyer while his uncle was being prepped for the trip in the ambulance, and Lucy sidled up beside him around two minutes past nine. She looked effortlessly pretty in jeans, heeled boots, a bright red sweater that clung to her curves and a fluffy white jacket. Her hair was down, flowing over her shoulders in a way that immediately got his attention.

"You're late," he said, grinning fractionally.

"I've been here for ages," she replied and crossed her arms, swinging her tote so hard it hit him on the behind. "Oh, sorry," she said breathlessly and then smiled. "The ambulance is about to leave, so we should get going."

Brant rattled his keys. "Okay."

It was cold out, but at least the snow had stopped falling and the roads were being cleared.

"Once you've finished renovating the Loose Moose," she said when they reached his truck and he opened the creaky passenger door, "you might want to consider giving this old girl an overhaul."

Brant waited until she was inside and grabbed the door. "Are you dissing my ride?"

She laughed. "Absolutely."

He shut the door and walked around the front. "That's cruel," he said once he slid in behind the wheel and started the engine. "I've had this truck since I was sixteen."

"I know," she said, and fiddled with the Saint Christopher magnet stuck on the dash. "You bought it off Mitch Culhane for two hundred bucks."

Brant laughed, thinking about how Grady had gone ballistic when he'd come home with the old truck that was blowing black smoke from the exhaust. The truck hadn't really been worth a damn back then, but he'd fixed it up some over the years. "How do you know that?"

She shrugged. "I think Brooke told me. We're friends, remember?"

He nodded. "I know that. She's another fan of yours."

"Another?"

"My mom," he replied, smirking a little. "Patron Saint *Lucia*."

Her eyes flashed. "How do you know my real name?" she asked as if it was something she didn't like.

"I think Brooke told me," he said then shrugged. "We're family…remember?"

"Funny guy," she quipped sweetly. "And I didn't think the Parkers and Culhanes were friends."

"Grady and I used to get into some scrapes with the Culhane brothers," he admitted wryly. "But since we shared a mutual dislike of the O'Sullivans we were friends more often than not."

"He still shouldn't have sold you this crappy old truck," she said. "You took Trudy Perkins to prom in it."

That's not all he'd done with Trudy on prom night, he thought, but he wasn't about to say that to the woman beside him. Trudy had been the wildest girl in their grade back then. And she'd had him wrapped around her little finger. He'd been a typical teenage boy and at the time Trudy had been his every fantasy.

But he'd changed. He didn't want that now. He wanted…well, he didn't have a damned clue what he wanted. All he knew was that there was nothing crass or easy about Lucy. She was kind and innocent. The kind of girl his mother approved of. Hell, the kind of girl his mother kept pushing him toward.

"I wonder what happened to Trudy," he said as he drove from the parking lot.

"She lives in Oregon. She married some rich banker and had three kids. I guess she could be divorced by now."

Brant glanced sideways. "How do you know this stuff?"

She shrugged. "I'm a doctor. People tell me things."

"Clearly."

"Except you wouldn't, right?" she said and leaned back in the seat. "You keep everything to yourself."

"Not everything."

"Everything," she said again. "Say, if I asked you what you were doing talking with Parker enemy number one, Liam O'Sullivan, the other night, you'd shrug those broad shoulders of yours and say it was *just business*."

"Well, it was."

She laughed softly and the sound hit him in the solar plexus. "When everyone knows he's trying to buy you out because he hates the idea of competition."

"Everyone knows that, do they?"

"Sure. He told Kayla and Kayla told me."

"Kayla?" he inquired. "That's your friend with the supermodel looks?"

"The one in the same. Every man notices Kayla. She's the original blonde bombshell."

Brant made a small grunting sound. "I've always preferred brunettes myself."

She glanced at him and then looked to the road ahead. "Could have fooled me."

Brant bit back a smile. "It's true."

"Trudy was blond," she said, frowning a little. "Remember?"

"She was brunette," he replied. "Trudy dyed her hair."

She snorted. "I'm pretty sure that wasn't the only fake part."

Brant wasn't one to kiss and tell, but the disapproval in Lucy's voice about the other woman's surgically enhanced attributes made him smile. "You could be right."

Lucy Monero had a habit of doing that. Whatever transpired between them, however much he desired her, wanted her, imagined kissing her, there was something else going on, too. Because he *liked* her. She was sweet and funny and good to be around. A balm for a weary soul. Something he could get used to, if he'd let himself. Not that he would.

"Incidentally," he said, speaking without his usual reserve. "Don't confuse my reluctance for disinterest."

"You really do talk in riddles sometimes," she said and then gave a soft laugh. "But I least I have you talking."

She did. In fact, he'd done a whole lot more talking with Lucy than he had with anyone outside his mother and brother and Uncle Joe for the past six months. "Communicating is important to you, isn't it?"

"People are important to me."

"I guess they have to be, considering your profession. Is that why you chose to become a doctor?"

She didn't answer and he glanced toward her and saw her gaze was downcast. She was thinking, remembering. Lost in some secret world of her own for a moment. She looked beautiful and just a little sad.

"No," she said finally. "It was because of my mom."

Brant could vaguely recall Katie Monero. She'd spoken with an Irish brogue and had taught dance lessons at the studio above the bakery in town. She'd married an Irish/Italian rancher who'd had no idea about cattle and horses, and who had died when Lucy was an adolescent. The crash that had taken her mother's life a few years later was a tragic accident. Katie had lost control of her car while a seventeen-year-old Lucy had dozed beside her. Katie had been flung from the car and Lucy had survived with barely a scratch.

"Because of the accident? It wasn't your fault, though."

"No," she said and sighed. "But my mom was alive for over ten minutes before the paramedics arrived. I didn't know what to do. I went numb. If I had put pressure on the main wound she might have had a chance. But I didn't know…and I vowed I'd never be in that position again. So I decided to go to medical school and become a doctor. I wanted to know that if I *was* ever in that position again that I would be able to do things differently."

"I understand," he said. "But you might need to let yourself off the hook a little."

"I can't," she replied. "I was there. I was the *only* person there that night. My mom needed me and I couldn't help her."

Brant's chest tightened. There was guilt and regret in her words. And he knew those things too well. "Sometimes you can't help," he said quietly. "Sometimes… sometimes in an impossibly bad situation, there's simply nothing you can do. You have to live through the moment and move on."

"It sounds like you know what that feels like."

"I do," he said soberly.

"But you don't like talking about it, do you?" she asked quietly. "The war, I mean."

Brant shrugged loosely. “No point rehashing the past.”

“Sometimes talking helps.”

He shrugged again. “For some people. Anyway, your mom…she’d be really proud of you.”

Lucy sighed. “I hope so. I hope she’d think I was a good person.”

“How could she not? You’re incredible.”

Heat crawled up his neck once he’d said the words. But there was no denying it. Lucy Monero was one hell of a woman.

“You better stop being nice to me,” she said softly, “or I might start polishing my white picket fence again.”

The heat in his neck suddenly choked him. “Look, I’m sorry about that, okay? I shouldn’t have said it. I must have sounded like some kind of egotistical idiot…and I’m not. I think I’ve just forgotten what it’s like to be normal. For years I’ve been driven by routine and rules, and now I’m living an ordinary life, talking about everyday stuff, and it takes practice. And time.”

“I know that,” she said and smiled. “I can’t imagine even some of what you’ve been through.”

His stomach clenched. “I had it easy compared to some. I got to come home. And in one piece.”

“I’m glad about that.”

He was, too. Most days. Until the guilt got him. The unforgiving, relentless guilt that reminded him that while he was home and healthy and physically unscathed, so many of his friends had not made it.

Survivor’s remorse. He’d heard about it. Read about it. Hell, he’d even had an army shrink tell him about it. But he hadn’t wanted to believe it. He longed to be grateful that he was still alive. But there were times when he couldn’t be. And there were times when he felt as though a part of him had died up on that ridge that day.

"So am I."

He tried to think of something else to say, some way to convince her that her mother would be very proud of the woman she had become, but she spoke again.

"Your brother thinks you have PTSD."

Brant flinched. "I don't—"

"You might," she said, cutting him off. "It can show itself in various ways. Do you sleep through the night?"

"Mostly," he lied.

"There are other symptoms," she went on to say, calmly, relentlessly. "Bad dreams, fatigue, isolation. I know Dr. Allenby would be available to talk to you. I can give you a referral if you like. Or make you an appointment."

Great, she thought he was a head case. A nut job. Weak. And he was pissed that his brother had been interfering. "Grady had to know I wouldn't be happy he'd said that to you."

She shrugged lightly. "I might have told him I wouldn't tell you."

"But you did."

She sighed. "I thought it was more important I tell you the truth than him."

"Why?"

Brant felt her stare from his hair to the soles of his feet. But he didn't dare look at her, because her next words should have rocked him to the core. But they didn't.

"Because it's not your brother I like, is it?"

Chapter Four

Lucy never imagined she would be sitting in his truck and telling Brant Parker she liked him.

Admit it...you more than like him.

To his credit, he didn't overreact. In fact, as the seconds ticked by, he didn't do anything. He simply drove, hands on the wheel, eyes and concentration directly ahead. Nothing about him indicated he was affected by her words in any way.

But as the seconds turned into minutes, her gratitude quickly turned into irritation.

Am I so completely unlikable in return?

She sucked in a breath, felt her annoyance build and crossed her arms. "Well…thank you."

"What?" he said and snapped his head sideways for a moment.

"Thank you for making me feel about as desirable as a rock."

More silence. But this time it was filled with a thick, relentless tension that she felt through to her bones. Okay, so he wasn't unmoved. But he wasn't saying much, either!

"Don't be stupid."

Lucy's jaw tightened and she glared at him. "Now I'm a *stupid* rock?"

"You're deliberately twisting my words to get some kind of reaction," he said, still not looking at her, still staring at the road ahead. "It's not going to work."

Lucy laughed humorlessly. "You know, Brant, you can be a real horse's ass sometimes."

"Around you?" He sighed heavily. "Sure seems that way."

"Okay… I take it back. I *don't* like you. Not one bit."

"Good," he quipped. "Let's keep it that way."

Lucy clenched her hands around her tote. "Fine by me."

Silence stretched between them like elastic. Lucy was about to shift her gaze sideways to stare out the window when she heard him chuckle.

"Something funny?" she asked.

"Yeah," he replied. "You are. We are."

"But there is no *we*," she reminded him. "Remember? I'm a hometown girl with picket-fence dreams and you're not marriage material… Isn't that how it went?"

His jaw clenched but she caught a smile teetering on his lips.

"Are you going to constantly remind me of every stupid thing I say, Lucy?"

"Probably."

"Don't know how we're ever gonna become friends if you keep doing that."

Lucy's breath caught. "Friends? You and me?"

He shrugged loosely. "Why not? It would sure beat

all that wasted energy I've put in trying to ignore you for the past six months."

She almost laughed out loud. Now he wanted to be friends after months of snubbing her very existence? The nerve of him. "So, you admit it?"

"Totally."

His honest reply quickly diffused her rising temper. "And now all of a sudden you want to be friends?"

"I want my mother to stop matchmaking," he replied. "I figure that if we're friends and she knows it's strictly platonic, she'll get off my back."

Lucy clenched her jaw. "Boy, you sure know how to make a girl feel good about herself."

"It wasn't meant as an insult," he said quietly. "On the contrary, I think having you as a friend could be the best move I've made in a long time."

She tried to smile. Friends? Sure. Whatever. "Okay, we'll be friends. To please your mom, of course."

"You're making fun of me," he said, his gaze straight ahead. "That's becoming something of a habit of yours."

"You could probably do with being brought down a peg or two."

He laughed and the sound filled the cab. "You think I need bringing down?"

"Sometimes. But I guess since you look the way you do…" Her voice trailed off.

"What does that mean?" he asked.

Lucy shrugged, coloring hotly and digging herself in deeper with every word. "You know…because you're so…so…"

"So?"

"Hot," she said quickly. "Handsome. Gorgeous. And if you had mirrors in your house you'd know that already."

"I don't spend time gazing at my own reflection," he said wryly.

Lucy smiled, pleasantly surprised to discover that beneath the brooding, indifferent facade he actually had a good sense of humor. "Here I was thinking all you pretty boys were the same."

His mouth twisted and then he laughed again. "You're making fun again. See," he said easily, "this 'being friends' thing is working out already."

Lucy laughed. "Yeah…it's a breeze."

The conversation shifted to more neutral topics other than their fledgling friendship and by the time they pulled into the parking lot at the hospital Lucy was in a much better mood. And it didn't take a genius to figure out that he had somehow diffused her temper with his deep voice and quiet small talk. So, he was smart. She knew that. It was one of the things she found attractive about him. There was an understated intensity about Brant Parker that captured her attention every time he was within a twenty-foot radius.

And now he wanted to be friends. That's all. And she'd agreed.

I'm an idiot.

What she needed to do was to stay well away from Brant Parker and his deep blue eyes and sexy indifference. Otherwise she was going to get her heart well and truly crushed.

They walked into the hospital side by side and once they reached reception Lucy quickly asked for directions to Joe Parker's room. Brant's uncle was sitting up in bed, pale and tired, but in good spirits.

"You're certainly keeping good company these days," Joe said to Brant and winked toward Lucy. "'Bout time."

Brant managed to look a little uncomfortable. "Dr.

Monero is here in case you have any questions about the tests you'll be having."

Joe patted the edge of the bed, inviting Lucy to sit. "Is that what he said, Doc?" He winked again, then glanced at his nephew. "Using a sick old man to get a date… shame on you."

"Uncle Joe, I hardly—"

"I insisted," Lucy said, smiling, certain that Brant didn't appreciate his uncle's teasing. "So this isn't really a date. I wanted to make sure you were okay."

Joe's eyes crinkled in the corners. "That's nice to hear. But all this seems like a big waste of time. I don't want a whole bunch of people sticking me with needles and poking at me. I feel fine."

"You had a heart attack, Uncle Joe," Brant reminded him seriously.

Joe waved a hand. "It was nothing, just a—"

"Mr. Parker," Lucy said gently as she perched herself on the edge of his bed. "You trust me, right?"

The older man nodded. "Well, of course, Doc."

Lucy patted his hand. "You're here because I thought it was the best thing considering what happened yesterday. And I'll be close by if you have any questions. So, promise me you won't cause a fuss and will do everything the doctors say."

He shrugged and looked toward his nephew. "She certainly has a way about her, doesn't she? Is she this bossy with you?"

Brant's mouth twitched. "Absolutely."

Joe laughed and it made Lucy smile. She knew Brant was watching her and feeling his gaze made her skin hot. She wished she wasn't so affected by him. It would certainly make getting him out of her system a whole lot easier.

Two doctors and a nurse arrived, and she shuffled off the bed and introduced herself and Brant. It took a few minutes for them to explain the testing and observations they would be doing over the next few hours and once Lucy was assured Joe was in good hands, she and Brant left the room.

"Should we stay?" he asked as they headed down the corridor.

"No," Lucy replied. "The less distraction your uncle has, the better. We'll come back in an hour or so. In the meantime, you can buy me a cup of herbal tea at the cafeteria."

Brant grinned slightly. "Sure, *Saint Lucia*."

She frowned. "I thought we agreed you were going to call me plain old Lucy."

"You're not old," he said as they reached the elevator. "And you're not plain."

Lucy's eyes widened as they stepped into the elevator. "Is that a compliment?"

He shrugged. "An observation."

She waited until the door closed and pressed the button. "Smooth," she said and crossed her arms. "But you obviously don't remember when I used to be a chubby teenager with braces and glasses."

The elevator opened and he waited while she stepped out before following her.

"I remember," he said, walking beside her as they headed for the cafeteria.

"And here I was thinking I was invisible back then."

When they reached the cafeteria he ordered her some tea and a coffee for himself and quickly found them a table. He pulled a seat out for her, waited while she settled in, then placed his jacket on the back of another chair and took a seat. “Are you always this hard on yourself?” he asked quietly.

Lucy frowned. “What?”

“You’re smart, successful…” His words trailed off for a moment and he rested his elbows on the table. “And beautiful. Why would you think anything less?”

“I don’t,” she said quickly, feeling heat rise up her neck. “I mean…not that I think I’m beautiful…because I’m obviously not. Well, not compared to someone like my friend Kayla. But I know I’m [illegible]”

“Being tall and blonde isn’t a trademark stamp of beauty, you know,” he said, meeting her gaze with a burning intensity that left her breathless. “There’s also beauty in curves and green eyes and freckles.”

I’m dreaming...that has to be it. There’s no other way Brant Parker would be telling me he thinks I’m beautiful.

She swallowed hard and took a breath. “Wow, you really can be charming when you put your mind to it.”

He chuckled. “I figure I have some making up to do.”

“You mean because you behaved like an idiot the other night?”

“Yes.”

She laughed softly. “You’re forgiven, okay? I’m not the kind of person to hold a grudge anyhow.”

“That’s very generous of you. My mother was right.”

Lucy’s expression narrowed. “She was?”

He half shrugged. “She said you were kind. And sweet.”

“Wow, how dull does that sound,” Lucy sighed.

Brant’s eyes darkened and he stared at her with a kind of hypnotic power. Awareness swirled through the space between them and she couldn’t have broken the visual connection even if she’d tried.

"Tell me something," he said so quietly that Lucy had to lean forward to hear him. "Why don't you have a boyfriend?"

Brant had no idea why he was asking Lucy Monero about her love life. He didn't want to know. The less he knew about the bewitching brunette the better. But he couldn't help himself. She looked so alluring with her lovely hair framing her face and her sparkling green eyes meeting his gaze with barely a blink.

She sat back, looking surprised. "A boyfriend?"

Her reaction was dead-on. It was none of his concern what she did or with whom. "Forget I—"

"No one's asked me out."

Impossible. Brant didn't bother to hide his disbelief. "No one?"

She raised a shoulder. "Not for a while. And I guess I wasn't all that interested in dating when I was in medical school. Since I've been back home I've been too busy at the hospital. You know how it is…it's easy to get caught up in work and forget everything else."

He *did* know how that was. Brant had deliberately focused on renovating the Loose Moose for the past month or so to avoid any entanglements. But something in her expression made him think there was more to it. "So there was no college boyfriend you left behind with a broken heart when you went to med school?"

"No," she replied. "I was a geek in high school and stayed that way in college."

He smiled, remembering how she'd always seemed to have her head in a book when she was a teenager. "Don't geeks date?" he asked quietly.

"Generally other geeks." She gave him a half smile.

"You know…when we're not sitting around doing calculus for fun or asking for extra homework."

He grinned. "You really were a geek."

"One hundred percent," she said and smiled at two nurses who passed close by their table. "It's how I got through high school," she said once they were alone again. "I hung out with my equally geekish friends, studied hard, avoided gym class and tried not to get upset when I didn't have a date for prom."

Her admission made him think of Trudy Perkins and the ordeal she'd put him through about prom. There was the dress, the suit, the limo she'd wanted him to hire and her displeasure at being forced to arrive at the event in his battered old truck—she'd made him crazy with her expectations and complaints. A week later they were done. He'd enlisted in the army and she didn't want to be with someone who wasn't going to be around. And he'd been happy about it. The last thing he'd wanted was to leave a girl behind when he went off to war. Not that Trudy was the love of his life. Sure, he'd wanted her…but it was little more than that. And she hadn't seemed heartbroken when they'd broken up.

Only sometimes, when he'd returned home in between tours or on leave, he'd wondered what it would be like to have someone waiting…to have warm arms and soft words to greet him. But there never was. He'd made a point of steering clear of anything serious. Hometown girls were off-limits. And now it was a complication he didn't need.

"Prom is overrated," he said and sugared his coffee.

"Easy for you to say," she replied and sipped her tea. "You probably had every cheerleader hanging off your every word during senior year in the hope you'd take them to the prom." She grinned slightly. "But in the end Trudy won your heart."

Brant smiled. "My relationship with Trudy had less to do with heart—" he saw her expression grow curiously "—and more to do with another part of my anatomy…if you get what I mean."

He watched, fascinated as color rose up her neck. She embarrassed easily, but wasn't shy about showing it. "Us geeks generally missed that class," she said, grinning.

Lucy had a good sense of humor and Brant liked that about her. He was discovering that he liked most things about her. She had a husky kind of laugh, for one, and it seemed to reverberate through him. And her green eyes always looked as though they held some sort of secret. There was an energy surrounding her, a magnetic pull that Brant found difficult to deny.

Over the past few months he'd deliberately steered clear of her. Of course, that hadn't stopped his attraction for her from growing. But he'd kept it under control, dismissed it, put it out of his mind most days. However, being around her now, sharing her company and listening to her soft voice, made it impossible to ignore the fact that he liked her. A lot. And it was messing with his head and his intentions. He'd suggested they be friends when it was the last thing he wanted. But if he made a move for anything else, he knew he'd make a mess of it. She was a nice woman. Too nice to fool around with. He wasn't a saint, but he wasn't a complete ass, either. If he asked her out, if they dated and started a relationship, she'd want more of him than he could give. And he wasn't ready for that. The truth was, Brant wasn't sure he ever would be.

"Thanks for coming today," he said and drank some coffee.

Lucy smiled. “No problem. I like your uncle. I like you, too,” she admitted. “Even though you can be an idiot.”

Her bluntness amused him and Brant grinned. “So… friends?”

“Isn't that what we already agreed?”

“Just making sure we're on the same page.”

“I don't think we're even in the same chapter,” she said. “You're something of an enigma, Brant. You're a good guy when you want to be, but underneath all that, I don't think you really allow anyone to see the real you at all.”

She was so close to the truth he fought the instinctive urge to get up and leave. But he stayed where he was and met her gaze. “Is that your professional opinion?”

She shrugged lightly. “That's my honest opinion.”

Brant drained his cup and looked at her. “If you've finished your tea we should probably get back to see how my uncle is doing.”

“You see, that's exactly my point. I've pushed a button by getting personal and now you want to bail.” She pushed her chair back and grabbed her bag. “You should talk to your mom and your brother,” she said frankly as she stood. “They're genuinely worried about you.”

He knew that. But he wasn't ready for an intervention. He wanted to forget. “I don't—”

“You can tell me to mind my own business,” she said, cutting him off. “But your mother trusts and confides in me, and I like her too much to dismiss her concerns. And your brother is concerned enough that he asked me to talk to you. If you don't want to discuss it with the people who care about you, at least make an appointment to speak with Dr. Allenby.”

She walked off before Brant had a chance to respond.

By the time he was on his feet and out of the cafeteria she was halfway down the corridor and heading for the elevator. When he reached her he was as wound up as a spring. He grasped her hand and turned her around.

"Have we stepped into some dimension where you get to tell me what to do?" he asked.

She didn't move, didn't pull away. Her hand felt small in his, but strong, and when her fingers wrapped around his, Brant experienced a pull toward her that was so intense he could barely breathe. The sensation was powerful and all consuming. He met her gaze and felt the connection through to his bones.

"Brant…"

She said his name on a sigh and he instinctively moved closer. Her eyes shone and her mouth parted ever so slightly. It was pure invitation and in that moment all Brant wanted to do was to kiss her. Only the fact that they were standing in a hospital corridor and people were walking past stopped him.

"I'll sort things out with my family, okay?" he said more agreeably than he felt as he released her.

"And Dr. Allenby?" she asked, relentless.

"I don't need a shrink," he said and pressed the elevator button.

When the elevator door opened she walked inside and Brant stepped in behind her.

"You know he specifically works with veterans, right?" she reminded him. "You were in a war, Brant. And you went through things a civilian like me couldn't possibly understand. But one conversation with Dr. Allenby doesn't mean you're his patient."

Brant ignored her remark and once they rode the elevator up two floors they walked out. Lucy's shoulders were tight and he knew she was upset with him. But he wasn't about to open up about anything. Not the war. And not what he went through. It was over. Done. It was the past and Brant was determined to live in the present… it was the very least he owed the men who had lost their lives on the ridge that day.

His uncle was awake and seemed happy to see them. Lucy discreetly grabbed the chart at the foot of the bed and glanced over it for a moment.

"As you can see, I've been poked and prodded." Joe grinned and then winked at Lucy. "Although I would've much rather you do the prodding, Doc."

"Uncle Joe," Brant said, frowning "That's not really appropriate to—"

"Oh, settle down," his uncle said and laughed. "I'm not seriously trying to cut in on your action with this lovely woman."

Brant shifted uncomfortably as heat rose up his neck. Uncle Joe had a wicked sense of humor and most days Brant found him amusing and enjoyed listening to his stories. But he wasn't in the mood for Joe's levity at the moment.

"Good," he said, seeing Lucy's brows rise slightly.

The cardiologist returned before any more was said and they spoke at length about his uncle's tests scheduled for that afternoon. Considering his history, the cardiac specialist made it clear that he would be keeping Joe at the hospital for a couple of days for further testing and monitoring, and to determine if he required surgery. Lucy asked several questions and Brant listened intently, thinking how grateful he was she was there.

Once the doctor left, Joe spoke again. "Now, I need a nap, so take this lovely young woman to lunch and let me rest."

He nodded. "Sure. I have to pick up some materials

for the Loose Moose while I'm in town, so we'll head over to Home Depot and come back later."

Joe already had his eyes closed and a minute later they were back in the elevator.

"If you have an errand to run I can hang out in the cafeteria," she said as they headed toward the ground floor.

"You'd prefer to be alone?" he asked as they stepped out of the elevator.

"Well…no, but I—"

"Let's go, then," he said and kept walking.

When they reached his truck, Brant opened the passenger door and stood aside for her to climb inside. He waited while she strapped into the seat belt and then closed the door. Once he was in the driver's seat, he started the truck and drove from the parking lot.

"Do you mind if we make a stop before lunch?" he asked. "I have the kitchen going in in the next couple of weeks and want to make sure the contractor has everything that I asked for."

"I don't mind."

Brant took a left turn. "So, how did my uncle seem to you?"

"Good," she replied. "The testing this afternoon will confirm how much damage was done to his heart from his attack yesterday. If he needs surgery he'll probably go in during the next few days. And if he does, then we'll speak with the surgeon together so you'll know exactly what will be done."

Her words calmed him. "Thank you. I appreciate your help with this."

She shrugged lightly. "I like Joe. He's a good man."

"Yeah," Brant agreed. "He's the best."

"He loves you a lot."

"It's mutual."

"You're lucky," she said quietly. "I mean, to have such a caring family."

"I know." Brant glanced sideways and noticed her hands were bunched tightly in her lap. He thought about her words and then realized how alone she was. "You must miss your mom."

"I do," she replied. "Every day."

He looked straight ahead. "I think… I think that sometimes I take my family for granted."

"You probably do," she returned bluntly. "But when you've always had something, it's easy to forget its value."

Brant bit back a grin. "That's very philosophical of you."

"I'm a deep-thinking girl."

She was a lot of things. Beautiful. Smart. Funny. Annoying. And kind. Lucy Monero was just about the nicest person he'd ever met. And if he had any sense he'd stay well clear of her and her knowing green eyes.

Yeah…that's what he should do.

That's what he *would* do.

Starting tomorrow.

Chapter Five

Tuesday was a long and emotionally tiring day in the ER and by the time Lucy pulled up in the driveway it was past six o'clock. Boots was in his usual spot in the front window and meowed loudly once she opened the front door and walked inside. She dropped her bag and keys on the sideboard in the hallway and walked into the kitchen. She needed a cup of strong tea, a shower and about an hour or two to unwind in front of the television.

Lucy filled the kettle, fed the cat and headed for the bathroom.

I look tired, she thought as she stared at her reflection in the bathroom mirror. Not surprising. Some days were harder than others. And today had been as hard as any ever got for a doctor.

Fifteen minutes later she was showered and dressed in gray sweats that were shapeless but comfortable. She pulled her hair into a messy topknot, shoved her feet into sheepskin slippers and wandered back into the kitchen. She made tea and left the bag in while she perused the contents of the refrigerator, quickly figuring she should have stopped at the grocery store on the way home. She was just about to settle on a noodle cup when her cell rang. It was Brooke.

"Hey, there," her friend said cheerfully. "How's everything?"

"Fine," she lied, thinking she didn't want to get into a discussion about her day. "Same as usual. You?"

"Okay. Spent the day repairing fences. And I had a dress fitting."

Brooke was a bridesmaid at Grady and Marissa's upcoming wedding. The event was only a couple of weeks away and Lucy knew her friend had been helping with the preparations. "Sounds like fun."

"It was more fun than I'd imagined," Brooke said then chuckled. "You know I'm not much into frills and frocks. I don't suppose I could get you to give me a hand with my hair and makeup on the day of the wedding? And Colleen wanted me to ask you if you'd help out getting the girls ready."

She meant Grady's three young daughters who were all flower girls. "Of course," she said and laughed. "Anything you need."

"Great," Brooke said, sounding relieved. "This is my first gig as a bridesmaid and I don't want to screw it up."

"You won't," she assured her friend who she knew was more at home in jeans and a plaid shirt than satin and high heels. "You'll do great. And just remember that—" She stopped speaking when her cell beeped, indicating an incoming call. "Hang on a minute, I have a call coming in. It might be the hospital." She put her friend on hold and checked the incoming number, realizing it wasn't one she recognized. "Hello?"

"Have you eaten, Lucia?"

Lucy stilled as Brant's deep voice wound up her spine. "Ah…no. Not yet."

He was silent for moment. "Feel like sharing a pizza?"

Pizza? With Brant? Was he asking her out on a date? *Maybe I'm hallucinating?*

"Oh…I…okay. But if we're going out I need to change my clothes so I'll—"

"No need, I'm outside," he said then hung up.

Seconds later there was a knock on her door. Lucy pushed some life into her legs and headed down the hallway. She opened the door and saw Brant on the other side of the security screen, dressed in jeans, a soft green sweater and his leather jacket, a pizza box in one hand and a six-pack of beer in the other. She fumbled with the cell phone and took Brooke off hold.

"I gotta go," she said quietly and opened the screen door.

"Everything all right?" Brooke asked.

"Fine," she said as he lingered on the threshold. "I'll call you tomorrow."

Once she ended the call, Brant's gaze flicked to the phone. "Am I interrupting something?"

"No," she replied. "I was just talking to Brooke. Um… what are you doing here?"

He held up the pizza box. "I told you. Dinner." His eyes glittered. "With a friend."

Lucy wasn't entirely convinced. "So this is not a date?"

She couldn't believe the words actually came out of her mouth.

He shook his head. "No, just a pizza and drinks. But

only if you like beer," he added. "I wasn't sure. I can duck out and get wine instead if you'd prefer?"

"I like beer," she said and stepped aside. His cheeks were pink, she noticed, as if he'd been standing out in the cold night air for a while. "You look cold," she said and ushered him inside and then closed the door.

"I'm okay."

"At least it's stopped snowing," she said and started walking down the hallway. "But the air has a real bite to it tonight. I think we're in for a long and cold winter."

"You're probably right," he said and followed her.

"I have a fireplace in the front living room that usually gets a workout every winter."

When they reached the kitchen he paused in the doorway. Lucy noticed his expression narrow as he raised a brow. "Well, it's all very circa 1975 in here."

She managed a grin. "I heard that retro is making a comeback."

"Not to this extent," he said about the gaudy color scheme and old-fashioned timber paneling. "It's very bright."

"It's awful," she admitted. "But I can't afford any renovations until next summer, so it has to stay like this until then. Wait until you see the bathroom," she said and laughed a little, feeling some of the tension leave her body. "It's baby pink, all over. My mom loved all things retro so she was very much at home here. Me...not so much. I've painted a few walls in the living room and bedrooms, but the rest will have to wait."

He grinned and placed the pizza box on the table. "I hope you like pepperoni."

Lucy smoothed her hands over her full hips briefly. "Do I look like a fussy eater to you?"

He laughed and the sound warmed her blood. God, he

had the sexy thing down pat. Even though she was sure he didn't know it. She'd accused him of being egotistical, but didn't really believe it.

"You look fine."

Fine? Lucy glanced down at her baggy sweats and woolen slippers. Good enough for friends, she suspected. Since he'd made it abundantly clear that's all they were.

"So, were all your other friends busy tonight?"

He stilled. "What's that supposed to mean?"

She shrugged. "Merely curious about why you're really here."

"I told you," he said, taking two beers and popping open the tabs. "Pizza with a friend. But if you need a more complicated reason…let's call it a thank-you for your kindness toward my uncle yesterday."

Lucy nodded slowly. "Did you see him today?"

"Yes, this morning. He's scheduled for bypass surgery on Friday."

"I know," she said and sighed. "I called the hospital this morning. I thought I would go and see him Friday morning before his surgery."

"I'm sure he'd like that," Brant said quietly. "I could meet you there. Or pick you up."

That meant more time in his company.

Being around Brant Parker was quickly becoming a regular occurrence.

Spending six hours with him the day before had worn down her defenses. Of course, she'd convinced herself the day had been all about his uncle. And it had been… on the surface. But after he'd finished his errands and they'd had lunch at a café a few blocks down from the hospital, Lucy knew there was a whole lot more going on. She still liked him. Too much. Despite his sometimes moody ways and indifference toward her over the past few months.

"Sure," she said vaguely. "I'll let you know. So, where do you want to eat? Here, surrounded by this lovely decor?" she asked, waving a hand toward the gaudy cupboards. "Or on the sofa in the living room?"

"The sofa," he replied.

Lucy grabbed the pizza box and read the writing on the top. "JoJo's? My favorite."

JoJo's Pizza Parlor was something of an institution in Cedar River. In high school she'd hung out there most Monday nights with her calculus club. Kayla had also been part of her group. The token swan among a group of ugly ducklings. The rest of the group had moved on or moved away, but she and her friend had never strayed too far. Once Kayla finished college in Washington State, she'd returned home, and Lucy followed a few years later.

"It's all in the secret sauce," he said and followed her down the hall.

Lucy smiled fractionally. "Do you remember how Joss Culhane got caught trying to swipe the recipe from old Mr. Radici one night after the place was closed up? He used to work there after school and told me how he wanted to get the recipe and duplicate it."

"I didn't realize you were so friendly with the Culhanes."

"I'm not," she said. "But Joss was hoping that since I was half-Italian I'd be able to help with the translation."

"And did you?"

"Not a chance," she replied. "My Italian is about as good as my Latin. He should have asked you," she said, placing the pizza box on the coffee table. "You speak a couple of languages, don't you?"

He shrugged lightly. "A little French."

She knew it was more than a little. Colleen had told her he was fluent. But he was being modest for some reason of his own. “Your mother told me that from your years in the military you also speak Arabic.”

“I speak some,” he said casually and came around the sofa. He placed her beer on the table and sat, grabbing up the remote. “There’s a replay of a game I missed on Sunday. Interested?”

Football? She’d rather stick a pencil in her eye. But she shrugged agreeably. “Sure.”

Pizza, beer and football.

They really were just friends.

If they were more than that, the conversation would be very different. She’d be in his arms, feeling his strength and comfort seep through her as she told him about her awful day. But she wouldn’t…because they weren’t.

Lucy positioned herself on the other side of the sofa and flipped the lid off the pizza box while he surfed channels with the remote. It seemed all too civilized. Like they’d done it countless times before. But inside she was reeling.

“You were a translator in the army, right?” she asked as she took a slice of pizza.

“Something like that.”

Her brows rose. “Secret stuff, huh?”

He carefully looked at the TV. “I prefer not talking about it.”

“I’m not trying to get into your head,” she said. “Just making conversation.”

He sighed softly and rested the remote on his knee. “Okay…then, yes. When I was in the military part of my job was to translate intelligence.”

“I thought they used civilians for that kind of thing.”

“They do,” he replied. “But there are times when the

front line is no place for a civilian. Part of my training included learning the local language and a few of the dialects."

"Because you have an aptitude for languages?"

"I guess," he said and fiddled with the remote.

"You were one of those people who breezed through high school without really trying, right?" she asked.

A pulse throbbed in his cheek. "You could say that."

"You would have made a good geek," she said, lightening the mood a little. "Well, except for the blue eyes and broad shoulders."

He turned up the volume a little and took a slice of pizza. "But I sucked at math," he admitted. "I still do. So I would never have made your calculus team."

Lucy shook her head, as if mocking him. "Shame… you missed some really exciting get-togethers where we discussed differential and integral calculus. Of course, you would have also missed out on having a date for the prom."

He groaned. "Are we back to that again? I told you, prom is overrated."

"Ha," she scoffed and took a bite of pizza. "So you say, Mr. Popularity."

He laughed and the sound filled her insides with a kind of fuzzy warmth that was so ridiculous she got mad with herself. *Just friends*. Remember that, she said to herself. She glanced sideways and observed his handsome profile. It was strange being with him…and yet, absurdly easy.

"I think you're confusing me with someone else."

"Really?" she queried. "Let's see, weren't you the quarterback with the pretty cheerleader girlfriend?"

"Are you trying to make the point that I was a cliché?"

"Nope," she replied and took another bite of pizza.

"You were too smart for that. But you did have a cheerleader girlfriend."

"It was over the week after prom," he said quietly.

"Was she mad at you for joining the army?"

"Kind of," he replied. "How'd you know that?"

Lucy shrugged. "Girls like Trudy are easy to read."

"But not girls like you," he said and drank some beer. "Right?"

She settled deeper into the sofa. "I've never considered myself easy on any level."

"No," he said, meeting her gaze. "You certainly aren't."

Lucy stayed silent as the space between them seemed to suddenly get smaller. There was such a sense of companionship in that moment…as if he knew her and she knew him. She took a deep breath and tried to concentrate on eating. And failed. She'd had such a bad day. One of the worse kinds of days for a doctor. A day when she couldn't do a damned thing to stop something terrible from happening.

"Lucy?"

His voice stirred her senses. "Yes," she said, not looking at him but staring straight ahead at the television.

"Are you okay?"

She shrugged and swallowed hard. Because he seemed to know, somehow, that she was barely hanging on. "I'm fine."

"I don't think you are."

She took a deep breath. "Today was just…a trying kind of day."

The volume of the television went down almost immediately and she glanced sideways to see he'd propped his beer and pizza on the coffee table. "What happened?" he asked quietly.

"You didn't come over here to hear about my bad day."

"No," he said honestly. "But I can listen if you want to talk about it."

Not in any stratosphere had she ever imagined that Brant Parker would be the kind of guy to simply sit on the couch and *listen*. She didn't want to think about how tempted she was to take up his offer. She *did* need to talk. Talking always helped. But this was Brant…and he wasn't the talkative type.

"I can't really—"

"Would you rather I leave?" he asked.

"No," she replied quickly, feeling emotion fill her chest. "I could probably use the company."

"Okay," he said and turned up the volume a couple of notches. "I'll stay. And we can eat pizza and watch football. Or you can talk if you want to."

There was something so earnest and at the same time so comforting about his words that she had to swallow back a sob. They were becoming friends. And friends shared things. After a moment she drew in a long and weary breath and spoke.

"The thing is… I'm a doctor. I'm trained to harness my emotions and, most days, I can cope with the bad things that happen," she admitted, twisting her hands in her lap. "But today…today was one of those hard days… when I have to wonder if I'm making a difference at all." She shifted on the sofa to face him and saw that he was watching her closely.

"What happened?" he asked soberly.

Lucy swallowed hard. "A woman came in to the ER today, six months pregnant, and I knew within minutes of examining her that she would lose her baby. There was no heartbeat and there was nothing I could do or say to comfort her and her husband." She stopped, took a breath and relived the moment again. “It was the third baby they had lost in less than three years. So, I’d witnessed their heartbreak before. And her husband…he begged me to do something…to help his wife…to save his son. And I couldn’t do anything.”

Heat burned her eyes and the tears she hadn’t dare allow that day suddenly came as though they had a will of their own. She didn’t stop them. She couldn’t have even if she’d tried.

“Lucy.” He said her name softly. “Sometimes you can’t do anything. Sometimes bad things just happen.” He grabbed her hand and held it, enclosing her fingers in a way that warmed her through to her bones. “You know that. We both know that.”

“I know it in here,” she said and tapped her temple with her free hand. “I know that, logically, I gave her the best medical care possible and nothing would have prevented their baby from dying. But it hurt so much to see their profound sadness. Her husband was hurting so much…hurting for the woman he loved and for the child they both desperately wanted. And I felt their pain deep down. I kept thinking, *This could be anyone...this could be me.* And then I felt like such a fraud because I’ve been trained to *not* feel.”

His gaze was unwavering. “You know, I think your innate ability to feel compassion and share that sadness is what makes you a great doctor. I saw the way you were with my uncle—and that kind of caring is genuine and heartfelt.” He squeezed her hand. “You’re not a fraud, Lucy…you’re kind and compassionate and amazing.”

And that was enough to send her over the edge.

She began to sob and suddenly she was in Brant’s arms. And he held her, tighter than anyone had ever held her. Lucy pressed her face into his chest, heard his steady, strong heartbeat, and slowly felt her sadness seep away. He pulled her against him and sat back into the sofa so she was lying across his lap, her hands on his shoulders, her head against his chest, her face pressed against the soft green sweater. She closed her eyes, took a shuddering breath and relaxed—in a way she never had before.

Brant had no idea what had made him land on Lucy's doorstep with a pizza and a six-pack. Or why he'd suggested they watch football in front of the television. Or why he'd taken her into his arms. But for the past half hour he had stayed still, holding her gently. She hadn't stirred. She lay perfectly still, her one hand resting against his chest, her head tucked beneath his chin. He was pretty sure she wasn't asleep, but she wasn't moving, either. Just breathing softly.

I should get up and hightail it out of here.

But he didn't. She felt too good in his arms. Her lovely curves fit against him in a way that was both arousing and oddly comforting. She was soft and womanly, and even though his arm was numb he didn't move. He couldn't remember the last time he'd sat with a woman and talked the way he'd been talking with Lucy. Maybe never.

She finally lifted her head and met his gaze.

"Okay now?" he asked softly.

She nodded and the scent of her apple shampoo assailed his senses. "I'm fine," she said as she pulled away. Brant released her instantly and she sat up. "Sorry about that."

He frowned. "Sorry for what?"

"Falling apart." She shrugged and crossed her arms. "I'm not normally so fragile."

"You had a bad day," he reminded her. "It happens."

She shrugged again. "Yeah…but I'm a doctor and I should be able to keep it inside. But thanks for understanding," she said and picked up the untouched beer bottle. "So, about this football game. Explain it to me."

"Explain football?"

"Sure," she said and drank some beer. "Why not? I mean, I'm not much into sports, but I'm willing to learn new things."

Brant smiled. "Actually, football should be right up your alley."

"How?"

"You like math, right?"

She nodded slowly. "Uh, sure. Geek to the core, remember."

Brant flicked up the volume and briefly explained some of the player's positions. "You see that guy there? He's the quarterback."

"Yeah…and?"

"And he's tracked by the percentage of completions attempted and made, along with completion yards. Plus, the distance he throws the ball and from which side of the field he throws it."

She raised a brow. "Still not following."

"These numbers are then used to develop a mathematical model of the quarterback, for statistical comparison with other quarterbacks. Just like the receiver who catches the pass is judged on the number of passes thrown to him and the number of catches. It's all about statistics," he added. "Math."

She grinned. "Gee, if I'd known how important math is to sport I would never have spent so much time trying to ditch gym class."

Brant laughed softly. "Wait until summer. Baseball is even more rooted in stats and averages."

"Good to know," she said and smiled as she took a drink. "Although, I'm not particularly athletic. I don't think I've ever swung a baseball bat."

"There's a practice net at Bakers Field, so if you want to learn, I could show you."

"I'll probably get stuck on first base."

The moment she said the words the mood between them shifted. He was certain she hadn't meant it to sound so provocative, but in her husky voice and with their close proximity, it was impossible to avoid thinking about it.

About her.

About getting to first base with Lucy Monero.

That was exactly what he wanted to do.

He wanted to kiss her sweet mouth more than he'd ever wanted to kiss anyone…ever.

"You know, I'm pretty sure I could get you off first base, Lucy."

He watched, fascinated, as color crept up her throat and landed on her cheeks. Despite her bravado, there was a kind of natural wholesomeness about her that was undeniable, magnetic and as sexy as hell. Her lower lip trembled and he fought the urge to see if her lips tasted as sweet as they looked.

He knew she was thinking it, too. Her green eyes shimmered with a sudden sultry haze that wound his stomach in knots and quickly hit him directly in the groin. He shifted in his seat, trying to get the thought from his mind.

"Wouldn't that…?" Her words trailed off and then she tried again. "Wouldn't that nullify the fact we're only friends?"

"Absolutely."

"And since you only want to be friends…"

"Yeah," he replied when her words faded. "That is what I said."

Her eyes widened. "Have you changed your mind?"

"About you? About us?" Brant dug deep because he had to. "No. Friends is best. Uncomplicated. Easy."

"Strange," she said as she placed the beer on the table and pushed back her hair. "This doesn't feel the least bit uncomplicated."

"You're right," he agreed. "I guess I'm new to this 'having a woman as a friend' thing."

She cocked her head. "What? You've never had a female friend before?"

He shook his head. "I don't think so. I mean…in the military? Yeah, for sure. But that was work. As a civilian? No."

"What about Brooke?"

"She's family so it doesn't count."

"Marissa?" she asked.

He shook his head. "She's my brother's fiancée and I'm just getting to know her."

"So, if you meet someone you like or were attracted to you'd what…sleep with her and then not see her again?"

Brant nodded slowly. "I guess."

She was frowning. "Sex means that little to you?"

Discomfiture straightened his back. He didn't want to talk about sex with Lucy Monero. He didn't want any part of his life to be under the microscope. "It's just a moment…a few hours…maybe a night. Little more."

She met his gaze. "Well, that explains why you're lonely."

Brant's back stiffened and he sat straighter. "I'm not—"

"Sure you are. Isn't that why you're here with me?"

Chapter Six

First base. Second base. Third base. Lucy was pretty sure Brant would have all the bases covered. The conversation was heading way out of her comfort zone. His, too, from the expression on his face. However she wasn't about to back down. He'd turned up on *her* doorstep, not the other way around.

"I am, too," she admitted. "Sometimes. I know I have my friends and my job, which I love...but the nights can get lonely. Or a rainy afternoon. Or a Sunday morning. You know, those times that people who are part of a couple probably take for granted."

He was watching her with such burning intensity it was impossible to look away. "I guess I don't think about it too much."

She didn't believe him. Despite his loving family and how close he was to his brother and uncle, Lucy knew he'd kept very much to himself since he'd returned to town. "Well, I do," she said and grinned a little. "I want to get married. I want to have a family… I mean, doesn't everyone need someone?" She stopped speaking for a moment and met his gaze. "Well, except for you, of course. You don't need anyone, right?"

The pulse in his cheek throbbed. "It's not about… needing someone. It's about knowing what I'm capable of at this point in time. And having a serious relationship isn't a priority."

"Define 'serious'?"

His mouth twitched. "The usual kind. Marriage-and-babies kind of serious."

"What if you fall in love with someone?" she asked, feeling herself flush again.

"I won't," he replied flatly. "I'm not looking for love, Lucia. Not with anyone."

Not with you.

His meaning was perfectly clear. And even though she was humiliated by the idea he thought she was imagining they had some kind relationship starting, Lucy put on her bravest face.

"Just as well we're only friends, then," she reminded him and focused her attention on the television.

"Just as well," he echoed and hiked up the volume.

He stayed for another half hour and when he left, the house felt ridiculously empty.

I'm such a fool.

Fantasizing about Brant was only going to lead to heartbreak. He'd made it clear he wasn't interested. So they'd spent a little time together and shared a pizza and a football game. And maybe she did collapse in his arms and hold on as if her life depended on it. And maybe he did hold her in return and give her the kind of comfort she'd only ever imagined existed. It wasn't real. *It wasn't anything.*

I'm not looking for love, Lucia. Not with anyone.

His words were quickly imprinted in her brain. Exactly where they needed to be. And what she needed to do was to stop daydreaming and forget about him.

Still, as she lay in bed later that night, staring at the ceiling, she couldn't help but remember his kindness. There was so much depth to him. More than he allowed people to see. He was strong and sincere and oozed integrity. But there was vulnerability, too. And pain…she was sure of it.

Something had happened to turn his heart to stone. She didn't doubt he'd experienced something terrible while he was deployed. Something he'd been keeping from everyone, even his brother and mother. And despite knowing it was madness to dig herself in any further, Lucy wanted to know what it was. She remembered how Grady had asked for her help. Clearly, Brant's family was genuinely concerned about him and Lucy had said she'd do what she could. Getting him to talk about what he'd been through in the military wasn't going to be easy. But the doctor in her felt a pull of responsibility to do what she could. And the woman in her wanted to understand his pain.

Her shift didn't start until eleven the following morning, so she slept in an hour longer than usual, then showered and dressed. Once she had a late breakfast she headed into town at nine-thirty to meet Kayla at the museum.

"You look tired," her friend said as they sat in Kayla's small office and began sipping on the take-out lattes Lucy had picked up from the Muffin Box on her way over.

"I didn't sleep much last night," she admitted, feeling the caffeine quickly kick in.

Kayla immediately looked concerned. "Bad dreams?"

She shrugged. "Just a long day," she said, deciding not to dwell on what had happened at the hospital the previous afternoon. "And then Brant dropped over with a pizza."

Kayla's eyes almost popped their sockets. "Really?"

"Yeah," she replied. "But don't read any more into it. We're just friends."

Kayla chuckled. "Sure you are."

"It's true," she said. "He's made it abundantly clear that he's not in the market for a relationship and I—"

"Won't meet anyone else if you keep hanging out with Brant Parker," Kayla reminded her.

"I know," she admitted. "But I like him. I have no idea why, of course. He's temperamental and indifferent and sometimes downright unfriendly. But…" She paused. "There are other times when he's such a great listener and he's really smart and funny and—"

"Oh, no," Kayla said, cutting her off. "I know that weepy look. You're actually falling for him. For real. This isn't high school, Lucy…you could really get your heart broken here."

"I know," she said as if they were two of the hardest words she'd ever said.

"Then stay away from him," Kayla suggested. "I mean it. He's quicksand for a girl like you."

"Like me?" she echoed. "You mean the oldest virgin on the planet?"

Kayla, Ash and Brooke were the only people who knew she'd never had an intimate relationship. Her friend smiled gently. "So, all that means is you haven't met the right man yet."

But I have.

"Why don't we talk about your complicated love life instead?" Lucy suggested. "What's going on with you and Liam?"

"Nothing," Kayla assured her. "My father would disown me, for one. And I don't like Liam O'Sullivan in the slightest. He's arrogant and opinionated and thinks way too much of himself. We're working on the museum extension plans together because he's on the committee and putting up most of the funding."

Lucy grinned. "Yeah, and I wonder why he's doing that?"

Kayla's cheeks colored hotly. "Because he knows how important the museum is to the town."

"Or because he wants to keep you in town," Lucy suggested. "Which probably wouldn't happen if the museum was forced to close down. You'd have to leave to get a job in a big city and Liam would be devastated," she teased.

Kayla waved a hand dismissively. "Enough about me. We're talking about you…and how you get your mind off Hot Stuff."

Lucy laughed. "Don't worry about me," she assured the other woman. "I'll be fine. After Friday I probably won't see him much at all and—"

"Friday?" Kayla asked.

"His uncle is having surgery," she explained. "I said I'd be there."

Kayla tut-tutted. "See…quicksand."

"I know what I'm doing."

I have no idea what I'm doing.

"I hope so. I'd hate to see you get hurt. And this thing with you and Brant has been going on for a long time and—"

"It's nothing," she assured Kayla. "Look, I know I was

all starry-eyed about him back in high school, and maybe I have talked way too much about him since I moved back to town. But I'm *not* pining after Brant Parker," she said firmly. "I promise."

Kayla's eyes widened. "So, if someone else comes along you'll give him a chance?"

She smiled at her friend. Kayla had been her wannabe matchmaker since they were kids. "Sure. As long as you do the same."

Kayla grinned. "No question about that. I'm a free agent."

"Yeah," Lucy agreed. "Except for being secretly in love with Liam O'Sullivan."

Kayla rolled her eyes dramatically. "Ha! Good try. I heard that his brother Kieran is coming to Grady and Marissa's wedding. He's a doctor like you…now that's worth thinking about. You guys used to work together in Sioux Falls, didn't you?"

"Yes. But no doctors," Lucy implored. "Too many long working hours."

Lucy stayed for another ten minutes, where they talked about Thanksgiving and the upcoming wedding. Lucy usually worked the holidays and this year was no exception. She would celebrate in a low-key way with her colleagues who'd either volunteered to work the holidays as she had or were unavoidably rostered. She really didn't mind working the holidays. It certainly beat sitting around her house alone.

For the first few years after her mother's death she'd tagged along with Kayla's family and they'd welcomed her wholeheartedly. But as she'd gotten older her need for inclusion waned and she was content to work and free up the time for her colleagues who had families.

But this year she felt more melancholic than usual.

When she got to work Lucy quickly forgot about her lonely life. A double vehicle accident on the highway meant half a dozen people were brought into the ER, two with serious injuries and another four with minor cuts and abrasions. She spent five hours on her feet and didn't take a break until it was close to five o'clock. She headed home a couple of hours later and pulled into her driveway at seven thirty just as rain began splattering the windshield.

Lucy grabbed her bag and made a quick dash for the house and was soaked to the skin by the time she got inside and shut the door. She shrugged out of her coat and flipped off her shoes, dropped her bag and keys in hall and headed for the bathroom. Fifteen minutes later she was clean, dry, and dressed in flannel pajamas and her favorite sheepskin slippers. She was just heading for the kitchen when she heard her cell pealing in her handbag. Lucy hot-footed it up the hall and rushed to grab her phone without registering the number.

"Hello?"

"You sound breathless," a deep voice said. "Everything okay?"

Heat rolled through her belly. "Brant, um, hi. Yes, I'm fine. You?"

"I'm okay. I'm calling to confirm Friday with you," he said evenly. "My uncle is really grateful that you'll be there."

Lucy's insides lurched. "Yes…well, I'm happy to do it if it reassures him. Only…"

He was silent for a moment when her words trailed. "Only?" he prompted finally.

She took a steadying breath. "I'd like you to do something for me in return."

The strained silence between them stretched like a

brittle elastic. "And what is that?" he asked after a moment, his voice raspier than usual.

Lucy knew she'd probably only get one chance to ask for what she wanted. So she went for it. "I'd like to make an appointment for you to speak with Dr. Allenby."

Brant fought the instinct he had to end the call and never dial her number again. But he didn't. He stayed on the line, grappling with his temper.

A shrink. Great.

And cleverly done, too. No demands, no subtle manipulation…just asking for what she wanted. He'd bet his boots she also had a great poker face. But since having her at the hospital was important to his uncle, he'd do what he had to do.

"Sure," he said easily, his heart pounding.

"Oh…great. I'll make an appointment for you."

"No problem," he said, ignoring the churning in his gut. "I'll pick you up Friday."

"Fine. See you then."

Brant disconnected the call and leaned back on the workbench. Damn, she wound him up! He shoved the phone into his shirt pocket and took a long breath. Lucy Monero was the most irritating, frustrating, demanding woman he'd ever known. He really needed to stop spending time with her before she got too far under his skin.

Too late.

He shook his tight shoulders, pushed himself off the bench and grabbed the circular saw. He had plenty of work to do before the plumbing contractors arrived on Monday. By his reckoning he had at least eight weeks' worth of work to do before he could open the tavern. In that time he had to think about hiring staff, including a chef and a barman. He wanted the place to be family friendly with good food and service at reasonable prices. Not as rustic as Rusty's nor as highbrow as O'Sullivan's, but somewhere in between. A place where he would be too busy to dwell on the war, the friends he'd lost or how he was irrevocably changed by all he'd experienced there.

And he longed to be so busy he wouldn't spend time thinking about Lucy Monero.

He turned around, plugged in the circular saw and picked a timber plank from the floor. All the booth seats needed replacing and he'd been steadily working his way through the task for the best part of three days. Brant measured out the timber he needed, grabbed the saw and began cutting through the plank. Within seconds the safety clip on the circular saw flipped back and the tool vibrated, jerked out of his grasp and bounced against the side of the work table. He quickly turned off the power switch, but not before the blade sliced through the skin on his left forearm.

Brant cursed loudly, dropped the saw and placed a hand over the wound. He was reaching for the small towel on the main bench when his cell rang. He grabbed the towel, quickly wrapped it around his arm, wiped most of the blood off his hand and pulled the phone from his pocket.

"Brant, it's me," said a breathless voice.

Lucy.

"Oh…hi."

"I just realized we didn't make a time for tomorrow."

He looked at the blood seeping through the towel. "I can't really talk at the moment. I'll call you back in a—"

"Why not? What are you doing?"

He was pretty sure she didn't realize how nosy she sounded. It made him grin despite the pain in his arm.

"Because I'm bleeding and I need to get a bandage on this—"

"You're bleeding?" The pitch of her voice went up a couple of notches. "What happened? What have you done this—?"

"An accident with a power tool," he said and then made a frustrated sound. "Look, I'll call you back when I—"

"Stay still and keep pressure on the injury," she said quickly. "I'll be there in five minutes."

Then she hung up.

It was actually six minutes before he heard a car pull up outside and about another thirty seconds before she tapped on the front door. Once she'd crossed the threshold he closed the door and looked at her. She carried a bright yellow umbrella, wore a brightly colored knitted beanie on her head and had a brown trench coat tightly belted around her waist. Letting his gaze travel down, he saw the pants she wore had tiny cats on them and she had slippers on her feet.

"Pajamas?"

She shrugged and rested the umbrella against the doorjamb. "I was in a hurry." She held up a black bag and looked at his arm. "I need to see what you've done," she said and glanced around. "And not here around all this dust. Upstairs. Let's go."

Right. Upstairs. He'd lived at the tavern for a couple of months and had not invited a single soul into the three-roomed apartment upstairs. Not even his mother and brother. It was sparsely furnished and other than the new bed, sofa and television he'd bought, about as warm and cosy as an ice-cube tray. Still, it served his purpose for the moment. He hesitated and then saw her frown and realized he wouldn't win an argument while she was in such a mood.

He nodded and walked toward the stairwell. "Don't expect too much."

"You're an idiot," she said as she followed. "I don't care where you live. Besides, you've seen my retro abode."

Retro and shabby maybe. But there was a warmth and peacefulness to her house that had made it very hard for him to leave her company the night before. It was even easier to recall how good she'd felt in his arms.

Once they reached the landing he stood aside to let her pass. She took a few steps into the living area and stopped. She clearly had an opinion about the place but unexpectedly kept it to herself. The room was spacious, clean and freshly painted, and was a combined living and kitchen and dining area. But he rarely used the kitchen other than to make coffee or to heat up something in the microwave. There was a small dining table and she immediately headed for it.

"Come here," she instructed once she placed her bag on the table and opened it. "Sit down."

He did as she asked and rested his arm on the table. She pulled a few things from the bag, including surgical gloves, and quickly put them on. He watched, fascinated as she gently removed the towel and examined the gash on his arm. Her touch was perfunctory and methodical. But having her so close made Brant achingly aware of every movement she made.

"So, how did this happen?" she asked as she stepped back, undid her belt and slipped off the trench coat.

Her buttoned-up pajamas were baggy and shapeless and did nothing to highlight her curves. But he was pretty sure she wasn't wearing a bra and the very idea spiked his libido instantly. And she smelled so good…like apples and peppermint. He cleared his throat and tried not think about how one layer of flannel stood between him and her beautiful skin. "I had a problem with a circular saw."

Her mouth twisted. "You certainly did. It's deep and needs a few stitches."

"Can you do that here?"

"Sure," she said. "But I don't have any local anesthetic so you'll have to be a tough guy for a few minutes."

Good. Pain would help him stop thinking about her skin and curves. She was so close that her leg was pressed against his. She'd ditched the beanie and, with her hair loose, her baggy pajamas and silly slippers, she was more beautiful, more desirable, than any woman had a right to be. And it aroused him. Big-time. He swallowed hard and concentrated on the pain in his arm instead. "No problem."

It took her less than ten minutes to stitch up the wound and wrap a bandage around his arm. "Try to keep it dry. And let me know if there's any irritation with the stitches. Seven days should do it before they need to come out."

"Okay, thanks."

"Is there anything else?"

She sounded mad. Annoyed. Angry.

And he was sure of it as he watched her clean up and thrust equipment back into her bag.

"Lucy?"

He gaze snapped toward him. "What?"

"You're mad at me?"

Her mouth tightened. "Yes, I am," she replied honestly. "It's like you have some kind of death wish. Motorbikes, mountain climbing, dangerous power tools… What's next, Brant? White-rapid canoeing? Skydiving?"

He laughed loudly and stood. "A defective power tool is hardly my fault."

"What about the other things?" she snapped.

"Haven't we been through this already? I told you about the bike accidents. And admitted I was an idiot to climb Kegg's Mountain without the correct gear." He grabbed her hand and stepped closer. "I don't have a death wish, Lucy. I promise you."

She looked up and met his stare head-on. God, he loved how she did that. Eye to eye. As though, for that brief moment in time, there was no one else in the world but the two of them. It felt like tonic. Like salve. As though her green-eyed gaze had the power to heal.

Of course she didn't…that was crazy thinking. But the more time he spent with her, the more difficult it was to keep denying how much he wanted her. Because wanting might turn into *needing*. And needing was out of the question. He couldn't afford to need anyone. And not someone as sweet and lovely as Lucy Monero.

"Are you sure? Your mom's worried you're… She's scared because she thinks you take too many risks. As if you don't care."

Brant's stomach tightened. His knew his mother frequently talked to Lucy, and it would be naive to think he didn't regularly turn up in their conversations. But he hated the idea that his mother was worrying about him unnecessarily. "What are you saying? That my mom thinks I'm reckless?"

"That's part of it."

His stomach continued to churn. "And what else… suicidal?"

She shrugged as though she didn't want to acknowledge the idea. "Maybe. It happens to soldiers all the—"

"I'm not," he said, cutting her off as he squeezed her

fingers. "I'm very happy to be alive and plan to stay that way for a long time."

"I hope so," she said, whisper-quiet.

Brant tugged her closer. "I promise I'm not depressed *or* suicidal."

She didn't look entirely convinced. "Depression can show itself with varying symptoms. Do you sleep well?"

"Mostly," he replied, hating that he was suddenly under the microscope but inexplicably unable to move away from her.

Her expression narrowed. "I don't believe you."

The truth burned his tongue. "Okay, so sometimes I don't sleep…sometimes I pace this room for hours or stare at the ceiling. That doesn't mean I'm depressed *or* suicidal."

"No," she replied. "Not on its own, but when you combine insomnia with other things, it can manifest itself into more."

"There are no other things."

"No?" she queried. "What about moodiness? Solitude?"

"If I was as disagreeable as you seem to think, I wouldn't be reopening the tavern."

"I didn't say you were disagreeable," she shot back quickly. "In fact, you're very charming and easy to talk to most of the time—like you were last night. I needed someone and you were there for me."

It didn't sound much like a compliment. Still, he didn't release her. And she didn't pull away. "But?"

"But you rarely, if ever, talk about yourself," she replied. "And that can be harmful to a person's well-being."

"So, I'm not much of a talker. That doesn't make me a head case."

She flinched. "Now you're angry. Being vulnerable

doesn't make you weak, Brant. Something bad happened to you over there, didn't it?"

His tone grew hard. "It was a war zone…bad things happened all around me and to a lot of people."

"I know that," she said, reaching up to touch his face. "But it's you I care about."

Her fingertips were warm, her touch electric.

His stomach dropped. Damn, she just about undid him.

Brant groaned. "Lucy…stop."

She didn't move her hand. "I can't," she said and then fingered the small scar on his chin. "How did you get this?" she asked, moving her fingertip to the scar at his temple. "And this?"

"I don't remember," he said vaguely and stared into her face.

Her cheeks were ablaze with color. Combined with her glorious hair and bright green eyes, it was a riveting combination. And he was immediately drawn into her gaze. Into the very space she possessed.

Brant moved his free hand to her nape and gently rubbed the skin at the back of her neck with his thumb. Her eyes widened immediately and a rush of soft breath escaped her. He couldn't have moved away even if he'd tried. She was pure temptation. Pure loveliness. And he wanted her. Brant wanted her so much it was making him crazy.

He said her name again, watched as her lips pouted a little in pure, sweet invitation.

Her hair tangled between his fingers and his grip tightened. She was looking at him, all eyes, all longing, and when he dipped his head, his intention clear, Brant heard a tiny moan escape her.

Her mouth was warm against his as their lips met.

She shuddered, half resistance, half compliance, as if in that moment she wasn't quite sure what she wanted. But it only lasted a second and then she relaxed against him. Brant instinctively pulled her closer. Her lips parted fractionally and he deepened the kiss, felt her shudder again before she opened her mouth to let him taste the softness within. It was the sweetest kiss he'd ever experienced, almost as though it possessed a kind of purity that had never been matched, or never would.

Brant suddenly felt as if he'd been sucker punched. Because he'd known, deep down, that kissing Lucy was always going to be incredible. Everything about her had been tempting him for months. Every look, every word, every touch, had been drawing them toward this moment. Toward each other. In that instant there was no denying it, no fighting it, no way he could have stopped himself from getting pulled deeper under her spell. And she felt it as much as he did, he was certain.

Her hands were now on his chest and then his shoulders, and he wrapped his arms around her, feeling her soft curves press fully against him. Her breasts, belly and hips pressed to him so perfectly her body was suddenly like a narcotic, drugging him mindless as the kiss continued and she tentatively accepted his tongue into her mouth in a slow, erotic dance that felt so good his knees weakened.

He pulled back when he needed to take a breath and stared down into her face. She was breathing heavily, as if she'd just run a marathon. And her green eyes were luminescent and shimmering with a kind of longing that heated his blood even further. He fought the urge to kiss her again. And again. Because he knew where it would lead. He wanted to make love to her so much he could barely think straight. He wanted to take her into his bed and peel off her silly pajamas and make love to every inch of her, over and over. He wanted to drug her mindless with kisses and to caress her skin until she begged for him to be inside her and then lose himself in her body for all eternity.

And knowing that she'd allow it was suddenly like a bucket of cold water over his libido.

He wasn't about to confuse her picket-fence dreams any more than he already had.

Brant released her abruptly and stepped back. "You should leave."

She moved unsteadily and gripped the table with one hand. "Brant… I…"

Her hurt expression cut through him, but he ignored it. "I mean it. Go home, Lucy," he said coldly. "I don't want you here."

Chapter Seven

It took Lucy about three seconds to grab her things and leave. She didn't bother getting back into the trench coat and instead had that and her bag clutched between her hands as she raced out of the room and down the stairs. She picked up her umbrella on the way and was out the door and back in her car so fast shc was out of breath and had a pain in her chest. She took a few deep breaths to calm her nerves as she buckled up and started the ignition.

And cursed Brant Parker the whole drive home.

Jerk.

She wasn't going to waste one more minute thinking about him.

I don't care if he is a great kisser.

Ha! She didn't have anything to compare it to anyhow. Perhaps he was a lousy kisser.

Yes...he's a terrible kisser and I never want to see him again.

Only...his kiss was incredible and the very idea of never seeing him again made her ache inside. And it confirmed what she'd suspected for weeks...she *was* falling for him. And it scared her to death. Because it was plain he would never return her feelings. He'd closed off that part of himself that was about emotion. It was a coping mechanism, she was certain. He'd experienced some trauma, something that had made him shut down. She'd seen it before firsthand...in herself. Right after her mother was killed and then in college when her roommate was raped. For years afterward she'd walked around wrapped in a kind of protective armor, never getting close to anyone, never letting anyone in. It had taken six months of therapy to help her heal and *only* once had she'd been able to self-reflect and realize she needed help. Brant was nowhere near that point. She knew it. And it made her ache for him.

Her lips tingled when she remembered their kiss. All her adult life she'd imagined that first kiss...what it would mean and who she'd share it with. In her most secret dreams she'd held on to the hope that Brant would sweep her off her feet and kiss her senseless. And for that brief moment he had...wholly and completely. And despite knowing it would probably never happen again, she couldn't and wouldn't regret it. Being with him, feeling his heart beat wildly beneath her palm, knowing he'd been as caught up in the moment as she had been, had fulfilled her every fantasy.

Still, she hurt all over thinking of his parting words.

Her cell rang and she let the call go. It beeped a few seconds later, indicating she had a message. By the time Lucy pulled into her driveway it rang again. She ignored it, got out of the car and headed inside. It took fifteen minutes to lock up the house, brush her teeth and hair and climb into bed. She stared at the cell phone for a good couple of minutes before she finally pressed the message button.

Brant's deep voice was instantly recognizable.

Her heart seemed to skip a beat. And then another.

"Hey…it's me." There was a pause. "I just wanted to make sure you were okay. And I'm… I'm really sorry about tonight. If you still want to come to the hospital on Friday I'll pick you up around nine." Another pause. "Thanks for the stitches. So…good night."

The message ended and she quickly let the next one play.

"It's me again." Another pause, longer this time. "It's just that a guy like me…can hurt a woman like you without even trying. Good night, Lucia."

Tears welled in her eyes a she ended the message and propped the phone on the bedside table. It was impossible to hate him. Even though good sense told her she should.

When she awoke the following morning she was weary and mad with herself for allowing him to invade her thoughts so much. She had an eight-hour shift at the hospital ahead of her and didn't need thoughts of Brant Parker distracting her while she was on the job. She had plenty of work to keep her busy and, when she had a chance, she made Brant an appointment with Dr. Allenby. She sent him a text message with the details and left out anything remotely personal. He replied with a brief thank-you text and she didn't respond further.

Thankfully it was a quiet afternoon in the ER and when she took a lunch break around two o'clock she spotted Colleen Parker sitting in the cafeteria. Colleen volunteered at the hospital a few times a month and was on the fund-raising committee. Lucy purchased a pot of tea and a savory muffin and walked across the room.

"Hello, there," the older woman said and welcomed Lucy toward her table with a friendly wave. "How are you?"

Lucy nodded, knowing she must look haggard and sleep-deprived. "Great. You?"

Colleen smiled warmly. "Very well."

"How's your brother-in-law?"

Collen nodded. "I saw Joe yesterday and he seems to be doing well, considering. I haven't seen you around much this week. Everything okay?"

Lucy shrugged and then nodded. "I've been busy."

Yeah...busy making out with your son.

"Not too busy for a cup of tea and a chat, I hope," Colleen said, motioning to the chair opposite.

Lucy sat. "Of course not. How's the fund-raiser going?"

Colleen waved a hand over the stack of files on the table. "I've been doing the rounds. We desperately need new recliners for the maternity rooms. You know, the ones that allow the new moms to nurse easily and new dads to sleep." She grinned ruefully. "But each one is a couple of thousand dollars and trying to raise that kind of money around the holidays is almost impossible. I may have to put aside my pride and ask the O'Sullivans to make another sizable donation."

Lucy knew Colleen had little time for the wealthiest and most influential family in town, given that they had treated her eldest son so poorly while he was married to Liz O'Sullivan, and often still did two and a half years after her death. But since they shared three grandchildren, she also knew Colleen remained civil and supported Grady's decision to keep his daughters in their lives.

"Maybe the holiday season will increase their generosity," she suggested.

Colleen made a face. "Nice idea. At least I only have to deal with Liam now and not the old man."

Lucy made a mental note to have a word with Kayla. Her friend seemed to have some influence with the older O'Sullivan son, despite her protests. "I'm sure it will work out. I'd like to believe that people *are* more generous at this time of year, so perhaps some of that holiday spirit will rub off on the O'Sullivans."

"Yes," Colleen replied, smiling. "You're probably right. So, how's your car? Brant said you had some trouble with it last week."

It was a subtle change in conversation and Lucy bit back a smile. Her car troubles seemed like an age ago. "Fine. I got a new battery and that fixed the problem."

Colleen's expression narrowed. "And I believe you're coming to the hospital tomorrow?"

"Yes," she replied, coloring when she realized Brant and his mother had been discussing her.

"That's very kind of you. Grady and I will be there, too. Marissa is watching the girls at the ranch."

Lucy would be surrounded by Parkers. But it didn't make her uneasy. She liked them all very much. Although the idea of seeing Brant again was tying her belly into knots. "I'm sure your brother-in-law will be fine."

"I hope so," Colleen said and looked unusually pensive. "Joe is a lot older than my husband and they were more like father and son than brothers. When Alan died," she said of her late husband, "Joe became both a father and uncle to my boys. He means the world to them, and to Brant in particular. I know he'd be devastated if anything happened to his uncle. And after what he went through on his last tour in the military… I'm scared for what this might mean."

Lucy saw the older woman's chin quiver. Usually, Colleen Parker came across as strong and self-assured and able to handle anything. But believing her youngest son was troubled was clearly more than she could cope with. And Lucy instinctively offered comfort.

"He'll be fine," she said and patted Colleen's hand. "Brant's been talking to me, starting to open up," she said, exaggerating the truth a little since Brant hadn't really told her anything. But Colleen needed reassurance. "He's strong, like you, and I truly believe he'll be okay."

"I hope so. And I'm glad he's been talking to you," she said, looking a little relieved. "As a child he was always much quieter than his brother…more serious. But he feels things deeply and that makes him sensitive, which is why he's such a good listener and a good friend to the people he's close to. When he chose a military career I knew he would give it one hundred percent of himself. I only hope he hasn't gotten completely lost in the process."

Lucy smiled. Yes, Brant was a good listener. "Like I said, I'm sure he'll be fine."

She wasn't about to discuss his upcoming meeting with Dr. Allenby. If Brant chose to tell or to not tell his family, then it was his business. She was a doctor, and although he wasn't her patient, she still had a moral and ethical responsibility to respect his privacy.

Lucy finished her tea and muffin, steered the conversation toward the upcoming wedding for a few minutes, and then left to return to the ER.

The next few hours were busy as a young man with a suspected spinal injury was brought in after he'd fallen off a horse at one of the local dude ranches while on vacation. He was immediately transferred to Rapid City for tests. Once he was on his way, a girl of eight with chronic asthma and very concerned parents came into Triage. As her shift was finishing she stitched up another boy who'd torn his earlobe on a fence.

She left around six. Once she was home Lucy fed the cat, showered, changed into sweats and made a toasted cheese sandwich for dinner.

She sat in the living room, crossed her legs lotus-style and grabbed her cell. She'd made a decision while showering to drive herself to the hospital in Rapid City the following morning. She didn't want to spend time with Brant in the close confines of his truck. The less time they spent together, the better it would be for her peace of mind. She sent him a text message to say she'd take her own car and then flicked on the television.

There was no point in pining over what could never be.

I don't want you here.

She didn't need to hear that again anytime soon.

He didn't want her in his apartment. Or his arms. Or his life.

And the sooner she accepted it the better.

For everyone.

Brant pulled into the hospital garage in Rapid City just after nine-thirty on Friday morning. His brother and mother were about twenty minutes away. They could have travelled together, but he was in no mood for chitchat and had opted to drive in by himself. Without company.

Without Lucy.

He headed for the surgical ward and stopped at the nurses' station to ask what bed his uncle was in. When he entered the room he discovered Lucy sitting on a chair beside Joe's bed, smiling at something his uncle was saying. He lingered by the door, watching her. She looked so effortlessly pretty in a bright green sweater and jeans. Her hair was down, framing her face. Her cheeks were flushed and her mouth looked fuller, softer… Just the idea of her lips against his made his gut churn. Recollections of kissing her, of holding her, bombarded his thoughts. Nothing had ever felt better and there was no way to erase the feel of her against him or the taste of her kiss from his memory.

She looked up as if she'd felt him standing there and their gazes clashed. It was electric. Powerful. If he'd had any doubts he'd been somehow pulled into her vortex over the past week, they disappeared. She was under his skin and in his thoughts. And he knew he was right to have sent her away the other night. If she'd stayed, they would have ended up in bed together, he was sure of it. They would have made love and then he would have been in so deep, Brant knew he would have no hope of pulling away from her without breaking her heart. Or his own. He didn't want that to happen. The closer they got, the more she'd dig away at him, which was out of the question. He didn't want anyone digging. He didn't want to see query and then sympathy in her eyes.

Because he would. She'd get him talking—that was her way. Everything he'd been through in Afghanistan would be out of the shadows and under the microscope. He'd be back out on the ridge again. Only this time he'd have no cover, no one watching his back, no one taking a bullet meant for him.

"You plannin' on hanging around the doorway all morning?"

His uncle's voice jerked him back into the moment. "No," he said and stepped into the room. "Of course not."

"Looks like you haven't slept for a couple of days," Joe remarked and frowned. "Everything all right?"

Brant nodded and didn't dare look at Lucy. "Fine. What time are you heading into surgery?"

Joe shrugged. "Anytime."

"The surgeon will make a final decision within the next half hour," Lucy said, pointing to the chart at the foot of the bed. "If the OBS are good, then it will go ahead as planned."

Brant moved toward the other side of the bed. Damned if he couldn't pick up traces of her apple shampoo in the air. He ignored it and started a conversation with his uncle, blindingly conscious of every move she made.

Grady and his mother arrived a few minutes later and he was grateful for the reprieve. His brother began talking to Lucy and while his mother chatted to Joe, Brant hung back and tried to ignore the sudden pounding at his temples.

Forty-five minutes later his uncle was wheeled from the room and taken into surgery. Grady and his mother took off for the cafeteria and Brant remained in the waiting room with Lucy. The room was small with half a dozen chairs, a small table covered with dog-eared magazines, a tea and coffee machine, and a water cooler. Brant sat at one end, Lucy at the other.

"Are you okay?"

Her soft voice echoed around the room. He watched as her gaze flicked from his face to his tightly clenched hands. Feeling her scrutiny, he relaxed his hands. "Sure."

"I know you're worried," she said quietly. "But the bypass procedure your uncle is having is fairly standard. I'm certain he'll pull through it without any problems."

Of course her words were comforting. That's what she did. She was a doctor—she knew how to phrase comfort and offer a soothing hand. But no matter how much he was tempted, Brant wasn't about to get drawn even further into her web.

"I'm sure you're right," he said flatly.

"And he wants to get out of here as soon as possible," she went on to say. "That's often the best motivator for a swift recovery."

"Sure," he said again and sat back in his seat.

Her expression narrowed. "How are the renovations coming along?"

Brant looked up. She was persistent, that's for sure. "You don't have to do this."

"Do what?"

"Try and take my mind off things. I'd prefer not to talk."

A spark seemed to fly from her gaze, as if she had an opinion but held it inside. He knew he was being a jerk. And that she was probably hurt by his words but was too stubborn to show it. It made him bite back a smile. Lucy Monero was full of opinions and passion and a kind of captivating intensity.

"Okay…fine," she said and pulled her cell phone from her tote as she shifted her eyes from his. "No talking."

Brant eased back into the chair and stared directly ahead. Within five minutes there was enough tension in the room to fill a stadium. He grabbed a magazine off the table and pretended to flip through the pages, but he was suddenly so restless he had to fight the urge to get out of his seat and pace. He could feel her, edgy and irritated just a few seats away. Her perfume lingered in the air and the way her fingers fiddled with the phone made him want to feel those hands on his skin. His attraction to her was relentless. Powerful. And certainly well out of his control.

"All right," he said, still not looking at her. "Let's talk."

She sighed sharply. "You're such a jerk."

He stilled. "Yeah… I know. I'm sorry. I guess I'm just worried about my uncle and–"

"I know that," she said, cutting him off as she dropped the phone back into her bag.

Tension tightened his shoulders. "So, did you switch a shift so you could be here today?"

Her head turned. "I start night shift tonight for a week so I didn't need to."

"When do you sleep?"

"Tomorrow," she replied.

He had a thought. "You're working over the Thanksgiving holiday?"

She nodded. "I usually do." Her gaze sharpened. "The other two doctors have families. So I work."

Brant considered her words. She had no family and gave up the holiday so that her colleagues could spend time with their loved ones. Her thoughtfulness made him like her even more. "That's very generous of you."

She shrugged lightly, but he wasn't fooled. She seemed a little sad. Strange, he thought as he looked at her, how quickly he'd gotten to know her moods. Like she'd gotten to know his. They'd developed a fraught, tense friendship over the past week and even though good sense told him otherwise, Brant felt compelled to get to know her even better. Despite her intriguing mix of strength and resilience, there were times when she seemed hauntingly vulnerable. And naive. Almost…innocent. Brant couldn't quite define it…couldn't work out what it was about her that drew him like a magnet. It wasn't just a physical thing. He'd been attracted to women before. But Lucy Monero was different. When he was around her it *felt* different. When he was around her *he* was different.

No...that's not it.

He was himself. Without armor. Without pretense. Without anything to hide behind. And that's why he'd avoided her since he'd returned home. The moment he'd met her again Brant had experienced a kind of heady awareness, deep down, that shattered all his plans to steer clear of involvement with anyone. When his mother had started matchmaking it was all the excuse he'd needed to act like a compete ass. And he had, again and again. On most occasions over the past few months he would barely acknowledge her when they were in the same room. Like a jerk. And a fool. And a coward.

"Lucy?"

She looked at him. "What?"

"I'm sorry about the other night." Face to face, the words were harder to say. "I didn't mean to, nor did I want to, hurt your feelings."

She shrugged. "You didn't. It was just a kiss, Brant. Nothing."

For a moment he thought she meant it and part of him was glad. But then she blinked and he saw the shimmer in her eyes. And in that moment he was done for.

Lucy was determined not to let him see her cry. She blinked a couple of times and willed the tears back. This wasn't the time or place to get all weepy. So they'd kissed and then he'd behaved badly.

Welcome to the world of being a grown-up.

"I did say that guys like me can hurt women like you without even trying," he reminded her. "And I'm not saying that to let myself off the hook. I genuinely don't want to see you get hurt. And if we get involved...you will."

Humiliation coursed over her skin. Was her sexual inexperience so obvious? Of course he must have noticed. No doubt he'd kissed many women over the years...like Trudy with her overt sexuality and bedroom eyes. No sweet wonder he'd acted like he'd wanted to run in the opposite direction after their kiss…he'd probably figured out she was a greenhorn in the bedroom department.

"Don't forget your appointment on Monday," she reminded him, quickly shifting the subject.

"I haven't," he said quietly. "Not that I think it's necessary. But I'll do it because I gave you my word that I would."

"He's a good counselor," she said. "He talks to a lot of the veterans at the home, including your uncle. So try to go with an open mind, okay?"

"I said I'd go," he replied. "And so you know, I have talked with a shrink before."

"Me, too."

His expression narrowed. "You have? Why?"

A week ago she wouldn't have dreamed of having such a conversation. But things had changed. They'd changed. Even without the kiss, things had altered between them. "It was a few years ago. I found myself withdrawn and spending way too much time alone. I knew I hadn't moved on from the accident and my mom's death and what happened in college so I—"

"What happened in college?" he asked, cutting her off.

Lucy took a deep breath. "Three weeks after first semester started my roommate was assaulted."

"Assaulted?"

"Raped," she explained and felt a familiar heaviness weigh down on her shoulders. "I found her and got her to the hospital and stayed with her for two days. She didn't press charges. She didn't tell anyone. She never went back to class and left school a month later."

She watched Brant's hands clench. "And the individual responsible?"

"He went about his life as though nothing had happened. I used to see him on campus and he always had a smug kind of sinister look on his face. He knew *I* knew what he'd done."

Brant got up and sat in the seat beside her. His back was straight, his shoulders tight. After a few seconds he spoke again. "Did he ever come near you?"

She shook her head. "I made sure I was never alone around him."

He looked relieved…as if the idea of someone hurting her was unthinkable.

She didn't want to imagine what it meant. She couldn't. Wouldn't. She was already halfway in love with him… Imagining he cared about her even a little was a catastrophe waiting to happen.

"And your friend?"

She shrugged. "We lost contact when I went to med school. I was still mourning my mom's death and with my course load and everything else… I don't think I had enough of myself to give. I think about her sometimes and wonder if she has had a happy life. Or if she let that one terrible thing outline the rest of her life. I hope not. I hope she managed to pull through and find some happiness. I still feel guilty, though… I still feel as though I could have done more to help her."

He grabbed her hand. "I'm sure you did everything you could."

Lucy's insides fluttered. Being so close to him wreaked havoc with her determination to keep him at a figurative distance. It was impossible when he was touching her. She wanted to pull her hand away but couldn't. "I hope so. But it reminded me of my mom all over again," she admitted, feeling a familiar pain seep into her heart. "I experienced the same helplessness, the same guilt. And yet, in a way, it confirmed my decision to go to med school."

He linked their fingers and held tight. "And look where you are now."

She glanced around. "In this room, you mean?"

"I mean," he said quietly, "that you're helping people again…because that's what you do."

Lucy's gaze flicked to their joined hands now resting on his jeans-clad thigh. "Looks to me like you're the one doing the helping."

"Don't kid yourself," he said and smiled so intimately it sent a shudder running through her. "The only reason I feel as if everything will work out with my uncle today is because of you."

As an admission it spoke volumes. This man, who she instinctively knew had been through hell and back and didn't want anyone to know it, trusted her.

"You know, it's hard to admit when we need help. Going to see a therapist was one of the most difficult things I've ever done," she said, feeling him flinch a little. But he didn't move his hand. The doctor in her suddenly made her cautious to get any more involved with him on a personal level. But the woman in her… She wanted to hold him in her arms and never let him go. "But I went because I wanted to feel whole again."

He expelled a heavy breath. "Whole? I don't even know what that means anymore."

"It means sleeping through the night," she said gently, looking straight ahead. "It means not waking up in a cold sweat at two o'clock in the morning. It means talking about what happened…it means sharing your fear."

"I can't."

Lucy heard the pain in his words but pressed on. "Why not?"

Silence stretched between them. Finally he spoke.

"Because I can't go back there."

Her insides constricted tightly. "Back where? To Afghanistan?"

He shook his head. "To that day. To that moment. To that second."

Lucy turned in the chair and grasped his arm. His muscles bunched beneath her touch. "Why can't you?"

"Because," he said quietly. "It will break me."

A sound interrupted them and they both looked toward the door. Grady stood in the doorway, two foam cups in his hand. Brant released her immediately and Lucy's hand dropped. She knew how it must have looked, being so close, their hands linked and her fingers digging into his arm. It would have looked impossibly intimate. Brant got to his feet and moved away, dropping into a seat by the water cooler.

"I brought coffee," Grady said as he entered the room. "It's not so great, but it's better than what comes out of that machine," he said and pointed to the equipment on the small counter. "Mom is walking around one of the gardens." He passed the coffee around and sat on one of the chairs. "So, what's new with you guys?"

Brant laughed first, because the question sounded so absurd considering Grady had walked into the room and caught them holding hands like a pair of guilty teens.

Lucy shook off her embarrassment and got to her feet. "I think I'll join Colleen in the garden."

She left the room and knew she would be the hot topic of conversation between the two brothers. But she didn't care. They could talk about her all they wanted. It wouldn't change the fact that she was falling in love with a man who was clearly so weighed down by his past he didn't have any room in his life…or his heart… for anyone.

By the time Joe came out of surgery it was past three

o'clock. Once she was certain he was out of danger and had come through the anesthetic, Lucy said goodbye to the Parkers. She was in the foyer, just about to walk through the automatic doors, when she heard her name being called.

Brant was about fifteen steps behind her.

"What?" she asked sharply, suddenly breathless.

"I wanted to thank you for being here."

"No problem," she said and clutched her tote.

"It means a lot to my uncle."

Lucy's brows came up sharply. "Is that the best you can do? Really?"

He thrust his hands into his jacket pockets. "Okay… if you need to hear it…it means a lot to me."

"Anytime," she said and managed a tight smile. "Make sure your uncle follows the doctor's orders. And good luck with your appointment on Monday."

She turned and began walking.

"Are you going to be there?" he asked.

He wanted her there? Did she dare? Her heart begged her to say yes. But her head told her not to make it too easy for him. Lucy nodded and tossed her hair. "I'll be around."

And then she walked out.

Chapter Eight

I'll be around...

Brant had been hearing those words in his head for three days.

Even with a busy weekend, traveling back and forth to the hospital to visit Joe, and then immersing himself in the renovation for the tavern, he couldn't get Lucy from his thoughts. He'd said too much. Admitted too much. And he couldn't believe he'd asked her if she was going to be at the appointment with him. No wonder she thought he was a head case who needed a shrink.

He lingered outside Dr. Allenby's small office at the veterans home five minutes before his appointment. He knew the doctor reasonably well and respected his abilities as a counselor. But that didn't mean he wanted to bare his soul to the other man. There was no one else in the office other than the middle-aged receptionist who kept glancing his way every time he moved.

Just over an hour later he was forced to admit that it hadn't been as bad as he'd expected. Dr. Allenby didn't try to force him to talk about the war. Instead Brant spoke about his uncle and the tavern and what it was like being back in Cedar River after so many years away. Of course, he wasn't entirely fooled. It was about gaining trust. Therapists employed tactics just as soldiers did. But at least Brant didn't break out into a cold sweat or completely shut down to the idea of conversation.

And he knew why.

Lucy.

He'd made a promise and he didn't want to disappoint her. Over the past week he'd seen enough hurt in her eyes and it was almost unbearable. Thinking about what she'd been through made him want to wrap her in his arms and protect her from the world. Of course he couldn't. He wouldn't. She wasn't his to protect. Besides, it sounded old-fashioned and foolish. She was a smart, independent woman who could obviously look after herself. Still…the thought lingered because imagining her hurt or in trouble somehow switched on something in his brain and made him feel protective and stupidly macho at the same time.

When he walked out of Dr. Allenby's office he saw Lucy sitting by the door, her head down, flicking through a magazine. He stopped in his tracks when she looked up and met his gaze.

"Hi," she said and placed the magazine down on the small table in the middle of the waiting area.

"Hi, yourself."

She got to her feet. "How did it go?"

He briefly raised one shoulder. "Okay."

She was just about to respond when the receptionist spoke. "Mr. Parker, will you be making another appointment to see the doctor?"

Brant's instinct was to reply with a resounding no. But he looked at Lucy and saw her gazing at him questioningly. As though she expected him to say no but hoped that he'd say yes. And, foolishly, he didn't want to disappoint her.

"Sure," he said, ignoring the heat filling his chest at the idea of another session under scrutiny. "How about the same time next week?"

Once the appointment was confirmed Brant thanked the receptionist and walked toward the door. He held it open and allowed Lucy to pass, catching a trace of her perfume as she moved ahead of him.

"So, it was okay?" she asked as they walked down the corridor.

"It was okay."

"I'm glad."

Brant slowed his stride a fraction. "I didn't think I'd see you here today."

"I said I'd be around," she reminded him.

His skin tightened. "I thought you were on night shift this week?"

"I am," she replied. "I changed at work and came straight here. I'll sleep this afternoon. How's your uncle?"

"Good," he replied. "He'll be home by the end of the week. Unfortunately not in time for Thanksgiving, but we'll celebrate with him over the weekend once he's back here. My mom is all about the holidays, so no doubt she'll make sure he gets some of her turkey and pumpkin pie."

"Sounds delicious," she said, smiling as she walked.

Lucy's heels clicked over the tiled floor. She wore a blue dress, shorter than usual, and her bare legs were impossible to ignore. Her hair was loose, flowing over her shoulders, and she wore a short denim jacket that accentuated the flare of her hips. And she had boots on, the short cowgirl kind with fringe on the side. For a moment he was poleaxed. He stopped walking and stared at her.

When she realized he wasn't beside her she came to a halt and turned around. "What?"

His gaze slide over her. "You look…really pretty."

"Oh…thanks."

Brant wondered if she knew how sexy she looked in her short dress and boots. Probably not. Most of the time he was pretty sure she had no idea how beautiful she was. "I appreciate you coming here today. It was very thoughtful of you. Especially considering that I haven't done much to deserve it."

Her cheeks colored and she smiled tightly. "No problem. Ah…how's your arm?"

"Good. No problems. You're something of a whiz with a needle."

"Yeah," she said almost breathlessly. "Shame I can't cook."

"Nice to know you have some flaws, Lucia."

The air between them crackled and he knew she felt it as much as he did.

"Well, I have to go," she said and swung her tote around her hips.

Disappointment foolishly rushed through him. "Hey, I was thinking we could have a late breakfast at—"

"I can't," she said, cutting him off. "I have a date."

A date?

He frowned. "Like an appointment?"

He watched her expression harden instantly. "No. Like a *date*. I'm not completely undatable, you know, Brant… despite what you might think."

"I've never said you were—"

"Goodbye. Have a good day."

How was he supposed to have a good anything when

she was out on a date with someone else? He reached for her and grabbed her hand. “Lucy…wait.”

Her fingers felt soft and warm enclosed within his. He met her gaze, saw her lip tremble a fraction and felt an inexplicable urge to pull her close.

“That’s just it, Brant,” she said, wriggling her hand free of his. “I’m tired of *waiting*.”

He watched her walk down the corridor, hips swaying, head held high, and fought the need to chase after her. He knew what she meant. It was a direct hit. She wanted more…and he didn’t know what the hell he wanted. Suddenly tired of his own company, Brant left the building, got into his truck and drove to his brother’s ranch.

The Parker Ranch was one of the largest in the area. His brother had been successfully running cattle for a decade and also worked as a county brand inspector. He’d always admired Grady’s work ethic and integrity. His brother was one of the most decent human beings he’d ever known. He’d been through a lot, too, with losing his wife more than two and half years earlier, and raising his three young daughters. Since finding love with Marissa Ellis, Brant knew his brother was truly happy again.

Grady was in the stables with Rex, the ranch foreman. Who, as it recently turned out, was also Marissa’s father. It was a long and complicated story, but Rex had returned to Cedar River after twenty-six years and discovered he had a daughter. Marissa’s mom had since passed away and Marissa had lived in New York, returning a couple of times a year to see her aunt and her best friend, Liz—Grady’s first wife. Yeah, complicated didn’t half cover it. Rex had stayed in town, gotten a job on the ranch and hoped he’d get a chance to connect with his daughter once in a while. Of course when Grady and Marissa had fallen in love, it had added a whole other level of complexity to the mix. But everything seemed to be working out. Marissa and Rex were getting to know one another, Grady's daughters were delighted by the idea of having a new mom, and his brother was head over heels in love with a woman who clearly adored him and his children.

Yeah…some people really did get a happy-ever-after.

Brant ignored the twitch in his gut and met his brother by the stable doors.

"Good of you to drop by," Grady said and clapped him on the shoulder. "The girls were complaining they haven't seen you for a while. You bailed on Saturday lunch at Mom's."

Brant shrugged. "I had stuff to do."

And he hadn't wanted to answer the inevitable barrage of questions he'd get from his mother about a certain brunette.

"Brooke's inside watching Tina," Grady said. "Coffee's on. I'll be a few minutes here."

Brant nodded, left his brother to his work and headed for the house.

He never ceased to be amazed by the sense of peace he felt whenever he walked into the ranch house. It was wide and sprawling, with verandas all the way around and shuttered windows. There was a love seat on the front porch area that he was pretty sure had been there for an eternity. Out the back was a pool and patio that Grady had put in a few years earlier.

The front door was open and he headed down the hall. His cousin Brooke was in the kitchen, chatting to Grady's youngest daughter, Tina. Brooke Laughton lived about as solitary a life as he did. She owned a small ranch out of town and had once been the queen of the rodeo circuit. That was before her parents were killed, her brother ran off and her fiancé left her for another woman. He liked Brooke, though—she was candid and easy to get along with.

As soon as the toddler spotted him she dropped the sippy cup in her hands and raced across the room. Brant scooped her up and held her close. She was a precious, loving child, and he adored her and both her sisters.

"Wow," Brooke said and smiled. "That was quite a welcome."

"I can be charming when I want to be."

She laughed and looked at the child clinging to him. "You know, that's a good look on you."

Brant shook his head. "Don't you start, too. I get that enough from Mom."

Brooke shrugged. "Just saying."

He dismissed his cousin's words. Mostly. But as he poured himself a mug of coffee and sat at the table while Tina proceeded to stack a pile of stuffed toys around him, he let the idea linger for a moment. Having a child was the biggest commitment a person could make. And yet he'd watched his brother do it seemingly effortlessly for years and a part of him had envied that ability. But every time he tried to see that future for himself the image always appeared blurred…as if he wasn't ready. Sometimes he wondered if he ever would be.

And then, deep down, a feeling suddenly stirred, a restless thought that quickly turned into something else…a picture…an idea. And if he closed his eyes for a second he could see it clearly…a woman and a child, both with dark curly hair and deep green eyes.

"Brant?"

His cousin's voice jerked him back into the present and he quickly dismissed the image in his head.

"How are things at the ranch?" he asked casually.

Brooke managed a smile. "Okay, I guess. I have creditors snapping at my heels and the land rezoning issue is still a problem. But I'm still there."

Brant knew his cousin had some serious financial concerns. "If there's anything I can—"

"There's not," she said quickly and then grinned. "So…you and Lucy, huh?"

"What?"

She shrugged lightly. "I hear things."

"You mean from Mom. I wouldn't believe everything you—"

"From Kayla, actually," Brooke said matter-of-factly. "She said you were there last week having dinner. Besides, Lucy is my friend…"

"And?"

Brooke's forehead wrinkled a little. "And don't break her heart, okay?"

Discomfiture spiraled up his spine. "I have no intention of doing any such thing."

"I hope not." His cousin half grinned. "Although you may have missed your shot."

"What?"

"Your shot," she echoed. "With Lucy. I spoke to her last night and she said she had a coffee date with Kieran O'Sullivan today. He's back in town for the wedding this weekend…you know how he's a friend of Marissa's. Anyway, he called Lucy last night and asked her out. I mean, it makes sense, I suppose, since they're both doctors so they'll have a lot in common. And they worked together at that hospital in Sioux Falls a few years back."

Kieran O'Sullivan. Great.

Not only did he have to think about the fact she was on a date, she was on that date with one of the Parkers' enemies. Well…maybe that was a stretch. Kieran was okay, considering he came from that family. They'd gone to school and been on the football team together. But *a date.*

The very idea twisted at his insides. But he didn't dare show it. "She's an adult. She can see who she wants."

Brooke laughed. "Gosh, you're a rotten liar. You're about as crazy as a bear in a trap just thinking about it." His cousin put up a hand. "But I won't say anything more about it. You're gonna have to figure this one out for yourself."

"What's he figuring out?"

Grady's voice from the doorway made them both turn.

"Lucy," Brooke supplied, still grinning.

His brother walked into the room. "Ah, the pretty green-eyed doctor with the heart of gold. Is he falling in love with her or something?"

"Looks like it," Brooke said and chuckled.

Brant jumped to his feet. "Would you two stop talking about me as though I'm not in the room? I am *not* falling in love with Lucy Monero," he insisted. "We're just friends."

"You looked pretty cozy together the other day at the hospital," Grady said then looked at Brooke. "They were holding hands. It was very sweet."

Brant's blood boiled. "We were *not* holding hands."

"Sure you were," Grady said and grinned as he winked toward their cousin.

"Sometimes you can be a real pain in the—" His words were immediately cut off when he remembered there was a child in the room. "I have to go. I'll see you both Thursday."

He bailed quickly, angry and so wound up he barely made it to his truck without tripping over his own feet. Sometimes families were nothing but trouble. He drove down the driveway and hit the main road into town.

By the time he'd settled his temper he'd pulled up at the back of the Loose Moose. And he got to work. It was still early, barely noon, and by three o'clock he'd finished building the new booths at the front of the tavern and was ready to start painting.

Is he falling in love with her or something? His brother's words kept slamming around in his head as he worked.

No. Absolutely not.

He was not falling in love. He didn't know how to. Lust, for sure. He wanted her like crazy. But love… That was out of the question. It was about sex, that's all. He wanted to make love to her. And, sure, he liked her. How could he not? She was smart and funny and kind and he enjoyed her company. But that was all it was. *Lust* and a little *like* thrown into the mix.

Not love.

That would be plain stupid.

Lucy enjoyed her coffee date with Kieran O'Sullivan. She liked Kieran and they'd always worked well together at the hospital in Sioux Falls. He was handsome and charming and had just enough of the O'Sullivan arrogance and confidence to make him good company. Of course, he'd never so much as made a blip on her radar. And they'd often joked about how they'd be perfect for one another—except for the fact they weren't attracted to each other in the least.

She left the café after accepting a chaste kiss on the cheek from her date and headed home. Once she was inside she fed the cat, changed into her pajamas, pulled the curtains closed to block out the light and dived into bed. She managed a few hours' sleep and by the time she roused it was past four o'clock. She ate a sandwich, had a cup of tea and spent an hour on her laptop paying bills and budgeting for the next month. She started her shift at seven and was just about to leave half an hour before when her cell beeped to indicate she had a text message.

Lucy grabbed the phone and checked the screen.

How was your date?

She sucked in a breath. Right. Suddenly, Brant Parker was Mr. Curious? She waited a few minutes and replied.

It was good. I had a soy latte and pecan cookie.

A minute passed and the phone beeped again.

Are you seeing him again?

Lucy stared at the screen. He had some nerve, that's for sure.

Maybe. Do you have a problem with that?

She waited for a minute, well aware that her provocative question would niggle him. *Well, he deserves a little niggling.* When a few more minutes passed and she didn't get a response, Lucy grabbed her bag, put on her shoes and headed out. It was snowing again and she covered her head with her coat as she raced to her car. She was just about to shove the key in the ignition when her cell beeped. She fumbled through her bag and pulled out her phone.

I think I do.

Lucy grinned foolishly.

I am seriously falling for this guy.

But she wasn't about to start imagining a few texts meant anything. Lucy fought the urge to write something in return and instead tossed the phone back into her tote. Then she drove into town and headed for the hospital.

It was a quiet but long night in the ER and when she got home at six the following morning she fell into bed after a quick shower and slept until noon. It usually took a couple of days for her body clock to kick in when she started a block of night shifts and this rotation proved to be more difficult than usual.

On Tuesday as she was getting ready to leave for work when her cell pealed.

It was a message from Brant.

How's work?

For a moment she considered ignoring him, but temptation got the better of her. She mulled over her response for several minutes and then replied.

Not busy. Which is good. Great to see you're keeping away from the place, too.

She grabbed her jacket and keys, and finished locking the house up. And waited for a reply.

Motorcycles and icy roads don't mix. Told you I wasn't reckless.

Lucy petted the cat, got into her coat, switched off the lights and headed outside. When she was inside her car she sent another message.

I guess you're not such a bad boy after all.

Ten seconds later he replied.

Lucia, I'm good. I promise you.

Even to her naive eyes the innuendo couldn't be missed and her body turned hot all over. She had so little experience flirting—*if* that's what they were doing—and didn't know how to handle the feelings running riot throughout her system. Of course she knew she wanted him. That one kiss had ignited her libido and she wanted to feel it again…and more. She wanted passion and sweat and heat and all the things she imagined were shared between two people who were lovers.

Because she wanted Brant Parker as her lover…no doubt about it. Only, she wasn't sure if that's what he wanted, too. Oh, he'd certainly kissed her that night in his apartment as if he was interested. But he'd also sent her packing. His hot then cold approach was confusing. And annoying. And *unacceptable*, she decided with a surge of confidence and gumption.

So by the time Wednesday evening came around and she was dressing for work, Lucy was almost back to being furious at him for behaving like such an impossible jerk.

Until her phone rang. She recognized the number and said his name almost on a sigh. "Brant…hello."

He was silent for a moment, and then spoke. "Lucia… I was wondering something… Do you think anyone would notice if I skipped the best man speech on Saturday?"

Lucy smiled to herself as the sound of his deep voice wound through her blood. She knew he'd never let his brother down like that.

"Yes," she said, laughing softly. "And you're an idiot for thinking it."

He chuckled. "Ain't that the truth."

Lucy dug deep. Making it too easy for him wasn't on her agenda. "Did you want something?"

She heard his hesitation. "No… I mean… I just wanted to say…that I think… I actually think I'm missing something."

Lucy's nerve endings twitched. Talking was much more intimate than texting and she could feel her nerves fraying. She took a deep breath. "Missing something in the speech you mean?"

"Not exactly."

"Then what do you mean?"

She heard him draw in a hard breath. "I miss… I think I miss…you. I mean, I think I miss talking to you."

God, he was impossible. "You think?"

There was more silence. "It's not…easy for me to say."

No…nothing was easy when it came to Brant.

She sucked in a breath, galvanized her nerves and spoke. "You're talking to me now."

Silence stretched again. "I guess I just wanted to see how you were."

"I'm fine. But I'm getting ready for work so–"

"Okay," he said quickly. "I'll let you go. Goodbye, Lucy."

She inhaled heavily. "Goodbye, Brant." She held the phone close to her ear. "And Brant…if you want to talk you know where I am."

By the time she got to work and swiped in, she was as coiled as a spring. Brant had a way of invading her thoughts like no one else. But she couldn't let anyone see that or allow her personal issues to impact her job. So she sucked in a few steadying breaths and got on with her shift.

She was about to take her first break around eight o'clock when Kayla unexpectedly turned up. Lucy met her by the nurse's station and gave her a hug.

"What brings you here?" she asked.

"I had a late meeting and was driving past and thought I'd stop by on the chance you might want to grab a coffee and have a chat."

A few minutes later they were in the staff lunch room, sipping coffee and tea.

"Don't forget my mother insists you stop by on Friday and have some Thanksgiving leftovers. She's pretty miffed you're not coming over again…you know how much my folks adore you."

Lucy was touched by Kayla's kindness. "I have to work a double shift. But I'll do my best to stop by, I promise. So, how are things?" she asked.

Kayla shrugged. "Same as usual. How's it going with Hot Stuff?"

"Would you stop calling him that?"

"I've been calling him that since the ninth grade," her friend reminded her. "I probably won't stop now. Is it true you were holding hands at the hospital last week?"

Lucy almost spat out her tea. "What?"

Kayla laughed. "Grady said something to Brooke. She told me. The great circle of life," she said and grinned.

"Circle of gossip more like," Lucy said, frowning. "And it wasn't *that* kind of hand holding."

"How many kinds are there?" Kayla asked, still grinning.

"Plenty," she replied. "We're friends and sometimes friends hold hands during a—"

"This is me, remember?" Kayla reminded her. "Your *best* friend. What's going on?"

"Honestly," Lucy said and let out an exasperated sigh. "I have no idea. Some days I feel like I'm back in high school again, as though I'm idly wasting my days doodling hearts with Brant Parker's name inside. Metaphorically speaking," she added. "I'm not really doodling. But I am spending way too much time thinking about him when I should be concentrating on my work, my home and my friends."

Kayla's perfectly beautiful face regarded her inquiringly. "And is he thinking about you, too?"

Lucy shrugged. "It's impossible to tell. Oh, he's civil to me now and we have spent quite a lot of time together lately and there's been a bit of texting this week so I—"

"Texting?"

"Yes," Lucy replied. "Texting."

Her friend chuckled. "That's kind of romantic."

"It's kind of confusing," she corrected. "And I can't allow myself to imagine it means too much. Even if I hadn't kissed him I probably wouldn't let myself believe it was—"

"Whoa," Kayla said, cutting her off as she waved a hand. "Back up. You kissed him?"

Lucy's skin heated. "Well, technically he kissed me," she explained. "And then I kissed him back."

Her friend's eyes widened. "And when were you going to share this tidbit?"

"Do you tell me every time you kiss Liam O'Sullivan?" Lucy teased.

Kayla groaned. "I don't kiss Liam. But enough about that—tell me everything… Was it fabulous?"

"Yes," she admitted and smiled. "You see, this *is* high school."

Her friend shook her head. "It's life, Lucy. So what happens next?"

She shrugged. "I have no idea. I'm new to all this, as you know. He keeps insisting he's all wrong for me—that I want a picket fence and he's not that kind of man. There's a part of him that's broken…or at least that's what he believes."

Kayla's eyes softened. "And can it be fixed?"

"I'm not sure he wants it fixed," she replied, exhaling heavily. "It's as if he's stuck somewhere…in some place, some moment in time, that he believes has suddenly come to define him. I don't know what it is and he's not talking. But I feel it whenever we're together. In here," she said and put a hand to her heart. "I feel as though he thinks he has to hang on to this thing from his past or he'll be *redefined*…somehow changed." She sighed and drank some tea. "Anyway, I really shouldn't be talking about him like this."

"Why not? It's only talking."

Heat filled her chest. "Because it doesn't feel right."

"Conflicting loyalty, hey?"

She nodded. "Something like that."

Kayla sat back in her chair and regarded her intently. "Lucy, have you considered that the reason you want Brant is because he *is* broken? Unfixable? Which also makes him unattainable?"

"That doesn't make sense."

"Sure it does," her friend said gently. "And it really means only one thing."

"And what's that?" she asked.

Kayla met her gaze. "That you're falling in love with him and it's scaring you to bits."

Lucy met her friend's stare head-on and knew she couldn't lie. "Yes…that's it exactly. I'm falling in love with a man who doesn't want to fall in love with me in return. And I'm terrified."

Kayla reached across the table and patted her hand. "So what are you going to do about it?"

Lucy sat back in her seat and tried to ignore the ache in her heart. "Nothing," she replied. "He has to figure this out for himself."

Chapter Nine

Brant stared at the huge cooked bird on the kitchen counter and impossibly bright vegetables piled onto a tray, and watched as his mother managed to attack three separate tasks at once without skipping a beat. Her skill in the kitchen never ceased to amaze him. She baked and grilled and sautéed like a head chef at a top-end restaurant and he suddenly had an idea.

"You know, Mom," he said and snatched a green bean from the plate. "You could come and work for me once the tavern opens. I'm still looking for a chef."

Colleen looked up from her task and smiled. "And have you bossing me around all day? I don't think so. Besides, I'm too busy to work. With the quilting club and volunteering at the hospital, I wouldn't find the time."

"It was worth a shot," he said playfully. "If you know of anyone worth interviewing, let me know."

Colleen grinned. "I hear chefs are a temperamental

lot. What about Abby Perkins? Didn't she study cooking in New Orleans for a year or so?"

"She works for O'Sullivan, remember?" he reminded his mother. Although he liked the idea of having a chef the caliber of Abby at the Loose Moose, he didn't like his chances of trying to poach her away from the O'Sullivans' five-star restaurant at the hotel. Abby had married Trudy's brother a year or so out of high school.

Brant had a couple of chefs lined up for interviews the following week and hoped to find someone from that. "So, how's the fund-raising coming along?"

"Slow," she acknowledged. "Although I did get a sizable donation from Liam O'Sullivan this week. Sometimes I think he's not as disagreeable as he likes to make out."

"Sure he is."

Colleen laughed. "Well, his brother is back in town for the week, so maybe that has something to do with his generous mood. Kieran always has been the peacemaker in that family."

Brant's shoulders twitched at the mention of the other man's name. "Yeah…maybe."

His mother looked at him oddly. "Everything all right?"

"Fine," he said, taking another green bean. "What time are the troops arriving?"

"Six o'clock," she replied. "You're the one who's here early."

"I had some time."

Her expression narrowed. "Something on your mind?"

Brant shrugged. "Not a thing."

"You're a worse liar that your brother," she said and smiled gently. "Grady will at least try and make a joke when he doesn't want to talk. So, have you seen much of Lucy?"

No...

And it was making him crazy. His brain was still scrambled by the idea of her being on a date with Kieran O'Sullivan. Texting her daily wasn't doing him any favors. Neither was calling her and saying he missed talking to her. He really needed to cut all contact to give himself a chance of getting her out of his thoughts. But he liked knowing what she was doing each day. He liked her sense of humor and how she didn't cut him any slack. He liked that they could share a joke or flirt or both and how it felt like the most normal thing he'd done since forever.

"Ah...not much," he said finally. "She's working over the holidays."

Colleen nodded. "Yes, I know. She's such a committed doctor. Everyone adores her at the hospital. But," his mother said, stirring the cranberry sauce simmering on the cooktop, "it's a shame she'll miss out on a real Thanksgiving dinner."

There was a gleam in his mother's eyes and Brant swallowed the tension suddenly closing his throat. "I'm sure they put something on at the hospital."

"Well, yes," Colleen said and nodded. "But it's not like a real home-cooked dinner with all the trimmings, is it?"

Brant didn't have a chance to respond because there was laughter and happy squeals from the front door that echoed down the hall. Within a minute his brother's family was bursting into the kitchen, with Grady behind them, his hands laden with bags. Marissa placed a Crock-Pot on the counter and moved around to help Colleen as the kids raced back and forth between Brant and Colleen, giving hugs and showing off sparkly nail glitter. Marissa's father, Rex, arrived minutes later and the kids quickly transferred their attention. There was lots of cheering and laughter and a kind of energetic happiness in the room that was palpable, and everyone looked incredibly content.

Everyone but him, he realized.

Grady slapped him on the back. "All set for Saturday?" his brother asked.

"Since it's your wedding," Brant reminded him, "shouldn't I be asking you that question?"

"I'm solid."

Marissa laughed. "Don't let him fool you. He's been a bag of nerves all week."

Grady groaned, swept her up into his arms and dropped a kiss to her forehead. "That is so not true. Don't believe a word she says."

As Brant watched their interaction, something heavy lodged in his chest. Although he was thrilled that Grady had found happiness, a part of him was almost envious. He'd never experienced envy before and couldn't understand it now. He certainly hadn't felt that way when Grady was married to Liz and had started a family. But things seemed different now. Back then Brant had been absorbed with his military career and hadn't had any time to think about relationships or having a family of his own. And, logically, he still didn't. However, in that moment, Brant didn't feel very logical. He felt…alone.

Lonely.

Which was plain stupid considering he was surrounded by the people he cared about most in the world. Still, the thought lingered as his mother shooed him and his brother and the kids to the living room while she finished preparing dinner. Marissa stayed to help in the kitchen and Brooke arrived about ten minutes later. It seemed strange not having Uncle Joe around on Thanksgiving, but he wasn't being released from hospital until the following day and the older man had insisted they all have their usual holiday celebration and not worry about him. Of course they all planned to visit him when he returned to the veterans home, but Brant missed Joe's corny jokes and craggy smiles.

By seven his mother called him in to the kitchen to carve the turkey and tossed an apron toward him when he entered.

"And slice it thinly," she instructed. "Not great chunks like your brother did last year."

Marissa laughed. "Don't let the master of the grill hear you say that, Colleen."

They all laughed and Grady popped his head around the doorway. "Too late."

Brant ignored the twitch in his gut. He should have been laughing along with the rest of his family, but he couldn't switch off the uneasiness running through his system. By the time the bird was carved and the table set, he felt so cloistered and uncomfortable he wanted to grab his keys and bail. Only his mother seemed to notice and once they were alone in the kitchen she asked what was wrong.

"I'm not sure," he replied honestly. All he knew was that he wanted to be somewhere else. He *needed* to be somewhere else.

Her expression narrowed. "Are you sleeping okay?"

Brant ignored the question and placed his hands on the counter. "Mom," he said quietly, "do you mind if I have dinner to go?"

"To go?" she echoed then frowned instantly. "You're leaving? But it's Thanksgiving."

Brant sighed. "I know and I'm sorry. But I think I need… I *feel* like I need to be somewhere else."

"Somewhere else?" Colleen's eyes widened and then her mouth slowly curved with a little smile—and a flash of understanding. "So, this dinner to go…is it for one or two?"

He swallowed hard, dismissed the heat in his face and spoke. "Two."

There was snow falling outside and enough cold air blasting through the hospital doors every time someone entered to remind the staff that winter was on its way. Thankfully it was quiet in the ER and even though they were on skeleton staff, by eight o'clock Lucy was ready for a mug of hot chocolate and fifteen minutes of watching a rerun of some mindless show on the television in the staff room.

She was just about to head that way when she was paged. Answering the call, she was told someone was waiting for her in the foyer. Thinking it was most likely Kayla coming to spread some holiday cheer, Lucy clipped the pager to her coat pocket and walked out of the ER and down to the general administration area. The place was deserted except for one of the maintenance staff pushing a janitor's trolley. She said hello as she passed.

And then she came to a standstill.

Brant stood beside the information desk, dressed in jeans, boots, a navy plaid shirt and sheepskin jacket. He had a Stetson on his head and carried a wicker basket. He turned as though sensing her arrival and immediately met her gaze.

"What are you doing here?" she asked, moving closer.

He held up the basket. "I thought… Thanksgiving dinner. For two."

"You brought me dinner?" Her legs suddenly stopped

working. "But shouldn't you be at your mom's? I know she was planning a big family—"

"I'm here," he said quietly. "With you."

Lucy almost burst into tears. It was the most utterly romantic thing anyone had ever done for her. Maybe even the kindest thing. She fought the burning sensation behind her eyes and tried to smile. "Oh, I…thanks."

His mouth twisted and when she stepped closer she noticed how a tiny pulse beat in his cheek. He looked wound up. On edge. Way out of his comfort zone.

And it made Lucy fall in love with him even more.

"Can you take a break?"

She nodded. "Sure. I'll just let the other doctor on duty know I'll be out of the ER for a while."

Lucy snatched up the closest telephone, put in a call to the nurse's station in the ER and said she'd be back in half an hour. When she turned her attention to Brant he was directly behind her and she quickly felt the heat emanating from his body. The edge of his jacket brushed her elbow and she looked up, caught in his gaze and without a hope of denying how pleased she was to see him.

"Where should we go?" he asked and looked around.

Lucy scanned their surroundings. The foyer was empty but still reasonably well-lit; there were a couple of vending machines against one wall and a small bench seat in between them.

"That looks like as good a spot as any," she said and headed to the other side of the room and sat.

He followed and sat beside her, placing the basket between them.

"It's quiet here tonight," he remarked, opening the basket.

Lucy peered inside and nodded. "It will probably get busier later tonight. Right now most people are eating dinner and celebrating. It's the MVAs or bouts of food poisoning that mostly keep the ER busy around the holidays."

He met her gaze. "Well, hopefully there's nothing poisonous in here."

She chuckled. "What are we having?"

"Turkey sandwiches on cranberry bread, sweet potato casserole and iced pumpkin cookies for dessert."

"Sounds delicious," she said and licked her bottom lip.

He pulled a few things from the basket and handed her a small stack of sandwiches wrapped in a gingham cloth. Lucy unwrapped the food and laid it on top of the basket while he bought sodas from the vending machine.

He sat, twisted the caps off the soda bottles and handed her one. "Happy Thanksgiving, Lucia," he said and clinked the bottle necks.

Lucy felt a surge of emotion rise up and fill her heart. "Happy Thanksgiving, Brant. And…thank you. I was feeling a little more alone than usual today."

"Me, too," he admitted and drank some soda.

Lucy passed him a sandwich. "But weren't you with your family tonight?"

Brant smiled warmly. "You can be in a room full of people and still feel alone."

He was right about that. "I feel that way, too. Sometimes when I'm at a party or out to dinner with friends, I get this strange feeling of disconnect. I especially felt that way after my mom died. For a long time I couldn't stand to be in crowds or around too many people at one time."

"It's a coping mechanism," he said softly. "But I understand what you're saying. You must think about your mom a lot around the holidays."

"I do," she said and sighed deeply. "She loved the holidays so much. And Christmas especially. She would decorate the house with a real tree and hang ornaments everywhere. And she and my dad would kiss under the mistletoe. There were always lots of gifts under the tree… Nothing extravagant, of course, since we didn't have a lot of money, just small things. Like, my dad would make her a footstool or she would bake his favorite cookies or knit him a pair of gloves that never really fit right. There was never much money but always a lot of love. And I miss that. One day I hope I'll have that again… if I get married and have children, that is."

"I'm sure you will," he said softly. "You're a marry-able kind of girl."

Her cheeks burned. "I hope I am. I mean, I hope there's someone who will want to marry me one day. Someone who will want to have children with me and grow old with me."

"Someone like Kieran O'Sullivan you mean?"

He sounded jealous and it made her grin. "I'd never marry a doctor. They work terrible hours. Besides, there's no blip."

"'Blip'?" he repeated.

"Blip," she said again and took a bite of her sandwich. "You know, on the radar."

His gaze narrowed and she could see he was trying to work out what she meant. "I believe a blip is a malfunction or a problem."

"Well, thank you, Mr. Walking Dictionary," she said, drinking some soda. "But falling in love *can* be a little problematic, don't you think?"

"I don't really know," he muttered and ate some food.

"I thought smart guys like you knew everything."

He glanced at her. "Who says I'm that smart?"

Lucy chuckled. "Oh, you're smart all right. Your mom

told me you've been asked to teach French at the high school in the evenings, for the adult classes."

He looked faintly embarrassed. "Yeah... I'm still thinking about it."

"Why are you so uncomfortable with the fact that most days you're probably the smartest person in the room?"

He shrugged again. "I could say the same thing to you."

"Oh, no. I had to study long and hard to get good grades. And I was hopeless at French and Latin." Her eyes widened. "Maybe you could teach me?"

"Teach you French?" He stretched out his legs. "Teach you how to French kiss, maybe."

Lucy almost spat out her sandwich as humiliation raced up her neck. "Was I so terrible that I need lessons?"

"Not at all," he replied softly. "You have a perfectly lovely mouth, Lucia."

She turned hot all over and tried to eat the rest of her sandwich. "This is really good."

"My mom is a good cook."

"She is. I should get her to give me some tips." Lucy's smile broadened. "And, just so we're straight on this, I'm not interested in Kieran O'Sullivan in the least. And it wasn't really a date, just two former colleagues catching up over coffee."

"Glad to hear it. The O'Sullivans think way too much of themselves."

She laughed. "He told me that his brother is going to keep trying to buy you out until you buckle under the pressure."

The pulse in his cheek throbbed. "Did he?"

She nodded. "And I told him he'd be waiting a long time."

He glanced at her. "Why did you tell him that?"

Lucy nodded. "Because I think anyone who has been a soldier on the front line for twelve years knows more about pressure and resilience than someone who sits behind a desk at a fancy hotel and barks out orders to employees all day."

He smiled and drank some soda. "I can handle Liam O'Sullivan…but thanks, it's very sweet of you to defend me."

"That's what friends do for one another."

He didn't disagree.

When he stayed silent Lucy spoke again. "Do you miss it? Being a soldier, I mean."

He nodded. "Sometimes I miss the code…the knowledge that someone always has your back. I miss the camaraderie and the friendship. Do I miss holding a weapon, using a weapon and dodging enemy fire? Not at all."

Lucy shivered. "I can't begin to imagine what you went through."

"At times it was hell on earth over there. A different world. But it was my job, so I did it the best I could while I was there."

"Why did you leave?' she asked quietly. "You were a career soldier, Brant. You're smart and could have worked in many different areas of the military… Why did you leave so suddenly and come back here and buy a burned-out tavern? It doesn't make a whole lot of sense," she said gently. "Unless something terrible happened that made you leave."

A shutter came down over his gaze. "I can't talk about it."

"You mean you *won't* talk about it," she corrected. "There's a difference, believe me, I know. I spent years refusing to talk about my mom's death and how I was plagued by guilt because I couldn't help her. But when

I did open up I stopped feeling guilty and experienced an incredible sense of freedom. It's like I'd been living in a house of glass, too afraid of what would break if I made a sound. But then I was out of this glass house and I could wave my arms around without breaking anything."

He twisted in the chair, placed the sandwich and soda into the basket and faced her. "Getting inside my head isn't helpful, Lucy. I'm only interested in living in this moment."

"This moment?" she asked. "Right now?"

"Right now," he replied.

"Is that why you're here with me…to be in the moment?"

"I'm here because…" His words trailed as he reached out and touched her chin. "Because the idea of *not* seeing you tonight was unthinkable."

Lucy's lip trembled. "And are you going to kiss me?"

"Yes," he said and took the sandwich from her hands and dropped it in the basket. "If that's okay?"

Her heart pounded behind her ribs. "It's more than okay."

His mouth touched hers gently, coaxing a response, and Lucy gave herself up to his kiss without hesitation. She waited for his advance and then invited him closer, loving how he now felt so familiar, so warm and strong, and how his mouth seemed to fit perfectly to hers. It was a chaste kiss compared to the one they'd shared in his apartment, and since they were in the hospital foyer and anyone could have walked by, Lucy was content to simply feel his mouth gently roam over hers. His hand stayed on her chin, steadying her, and she kissed him back softly, loving the connection, loving the moment. Loving him.

"Lucy…" He suddenly spoke her name in a kind of

agonized whisper. "When your shift is over, come back to my apartment."

"Brant, I—"

"I want to make love to you," he said, trailing his mouth down her jaw. "You're all I can think about."

His words were like music to her ears. He wanted her. She wanted him. It should have been as simple as that. But it wasn't.

"I want that, too…so much."

He clearly heard the reluctance in her voice because he pulled back. "But?"

"But not until you talk to me. Really talk."

"Talk?"

She swallowed hard. "About your past."

He released her and was on his feet in two seconds flat. "Blackmail? Really?"

"Not blackmail," she said in defense. "If I'm going to *be* with someone, I'd like to know who he is."

He frowned. "You know me already."

"I know what you allow people to see," she said. "I know there are things about you that you keep deep inside and are afraid to let anyone see. Including me."

"There's not."

Lucy didn't back down. "I may be naive, Brant, but I'm not gullible. I want to be with you. But I want to get to know you, too. What you think, what you feel." She put a hand to her heart. "In here. And that includes knowing what you went through when you were—"

"How has you and I sleeping together got anything to do with what happened when I was in the military?" he asked, cutting her off.

"It just does."

"No," he said irritably. "This is simply some kind of female manipulation."

"It's not," she implored. "I'm not like that. And there's nothing simple about this."

"How's this for simple?" he shot back. "You want to know about my past because you want to *fix* me. Well, I'm not some kind of renovation project for you, Lucy. I don't need *fixing*. Save that for your patients."

He turned around and walked away, his straight back and tight limbs making his anger abundantly clear.

Lucy watched as he disappeared through the doors and a blast of cold air rushed through the foyer. Her heart sank miserably and she packed up the basket beside her. So much for a romantic dinner for two.

Lucy grabbed the basket, let out a long, unhappy breath, and walked back to the ER.

The Parker-Ellis wedding was being held at Grady's ranch. However, Lucy had stopped by Marissa's place, which was next door to Grady's, to help Brooke and Colleen get the kids ready for the ceremony.

She braided their hair and the three little girls looked so adorable in their lavender-and-ivory dresses. Lucy was a little misty-eyed when she saw how beautiful Marissa was in her lace wedding gown. The other woman positively glowed. Even Brooke, who was as tough as the most ornery cowboy, had a tiny tear in her eye. One day Lucy hoped to be a bride herself. *One day.* When she was over her foolish infatuation with Brant Parker.

She left with Colleen and the kids and took a seat at the back of the ceremony next to her friend Ash. The huge tent had been beautifully decorated, and heaters were discreetly in place to keep the area warm and comfortable for the guests. The white-covered chairs with lavender tulle bows had been laid out in aisle format and, even from the back, she had a great view of the altar. And of Brant.

He stood beside his brother as best man, dressed in a gray suit, white shirt and bolo tie. He looked so handsome. But tense. His jaw was tight and his back straight. And she couldn't take her eyes off him. He turned when the music started and their gazes clashed. In the past two days she'd gone from loving him to hating him, back to loving him and then hating him again.

As she met his gaze head-on and realized he wasn't looking at the bride as she walked down the aisle, as everyone else was, but that he was looking at *her*, Lucy's skin burned from head to toe.

Once Marissa reached the altar, everyone turned to the front. The service was moving and heartfelt, and Lucy wiped tears from her cheeks once the celebrant pronounced them as husband and wife. Grady's daughters were jumping around excitedly as he kissed his bride and the guests erupted into applause they walked back down the aisle. Brant followed with Brooke on his arm and he flipped her a look that was so blisteringly intense as he passed that Ash jabbed her in the ribs.

"Wow," her friend whispered. "What on earth is going on between you two?"

"Nothing," she replied and watched as he escorted Brooke from the tent. It was a gloriously cool but clear day and the wedding party headed out for the photographs to be taken. "It's a long story."

"I like long stories," Ash said as they moved from the seating area toward the other side of the tent where a dozen large round tables were set up with crisp linen and white dinnerware. It was elegant and understated and exactly what a wedding should be, she thought as they wove their way through the tables to find their seats.

But Lucy didn't tell the story. She wasn't in the mood for any kind of post mortem about her aborted relationship with Brant. Because she was pretty sure it was over. Well, whatever they had was over. He'd made no contact for two days and she hadn't garnered the courage to call him, either.

By the time the wedding party returned it was time to be seated for dinner and then the speeches began. If she'd imagined Brant would be nervous giving his speech, she was mistaken. He was charming and funny, sharing anecdotes about his brother that made the audience laugh, and at the end there was a toast and applause.

Then later the bride and groom hit the dance floor and swayed to an old Garth Brooks love song that was so sentimental Lucy wanted to burst into tears. Seeing Grady and Marissa together was seeing real love, firsthand. They'd somehow managed to find one another despite the obstacles they had endured and made a lifetime commitment. She envied them. And felt a little sad for herself.

She looked around and noticed Brant dancing with Brooke. More couples were on the dance floor. Since Ash had been chatting with Kieran for the past hour Lucy was now conspicuously alone at her table. A band of tension tightened around her forehead and she grimaced. The last thing she wanted was a headache.

She needed aspirin so she got up, left the tent and headed around to the back of the house. Lucy let herself through the gate and walked in through the back door. She could still hear the music and laughter coming from the tent, but the house was deserted. She'd been to the ranch several times and knew her way around, so she made her way down the hall toward the main bathroom.

She was just about to open the top vanity cupboard when she heard Brant's voice behind her.

"Everything okay, Lucy?"

She swiveled on her heels. "Fine," she said breathlessly. "I was hoping to find some aspirin."

He frowned. "Kitchen. Pantry. Top shelf." He grabbed her hand. "Come on, I'll get it for you."

Heat coursed over her skin at his touch and she longed for the strength to pull away. But he held her firm and led her down the hall and toward the huge kitchen. When he released her she crossed her arms and waited while he opened the pantry and took out a small container of painkillers. He filled a glass with water and placed both items on the counter.

"Thanks," she said and took the medication.

"Headache?"

"Almost," she replied. "Just getting it before it gets me. So, how's your uncle?"

He shrugged lightly. "He seemed okay when I saw him this morning."

"I checked on him yesterday afternoon and he seems to be recovering quite well."

"I hope so." He rested his hip on the counter. "He was miffed that he missed this today. So, are you enjoying the wedding?"

"Sure," she said, placing the glass down. "You?"

His mouth twisted. "Sure." He met her gaze. "That's why we're both in here."

"I was looking for aspirin," she said and shrugged. "What's your excuse?"

"I was looking for you."

Her heart skipped a beat and she was suddenly absorbed by him. "Why?"

"You know why."

His deep voice resonated around the room and even though she was desperate to leave, she couldn't. "I *don't* know. You're confusing me, Brant. Nothing has changed since the other night."

She was right to say it. Right to remind him.

His gaze darkened as he looked her over. "You look so beautiful in that dress."

The long-sleeved deep red soft jersey dress molded to her breasts and waist and flared out over her hips. She'd had it in her closet for two years with rarely an occasion to wear it. Sometimes she wondered if it was going to gather dust along with her old prom dress. "Thanks. You look pretty good yourself. It still doesn't change anything."

Silence stretched between them and Lucy was so caught up, so hypnotized by his dark blue eyes, she couldn't move. Couldn't think. She could only feel. He looked lost and alone, and she remembered how he'd accused her of wanting to *fix* him. And she did. She longed to make him whole again. Because she knew he would make her whole in return.

"Okay," he said finally, as though it was one of the hardest words he'd ever spoken. "I'll tell you. I don't know why I want to tell you. I don't know what it is about you that makes me want to talk about things that I try not to think about. But for the past two days all I've been able to think about is you when I should be doing a hundred other things."

Lucy's breath caught in her throat. She waited. The silence was agonizing. The hollow, haunted look in his eyes made her ache inside and when he spoke again her heart just about broke into pieces.

"Three men in my unit died," he said quietly, his voice little more than a husky whisper. "And they died because of me."

Chapter Ten

Brant knew there was no taking back the words once they were out. He'd kept them inside for over a year, never daring to say them out loud. It should have felt good. Cathartic. Instead, every morsel of guilt and regret he'd felt since that day came rushing back and almost knocked him over.

Three men—whose names would be forever etched into his blood and bones and his very soul—had died to save him.

"Tell me what happened."

Lucy's voice, soft and concerned. A voice that haunted his dreams and consumed his waking hours. When good sense told him to stay away, he was inexplicably drawn even more toward her. When everyone else made him clam up, Lucy Monero did the opposite. Talking to her was, somehow, salvation.

"They were protecting me," he said flatly.

Her gaze narrowed. "I don't understand."

"I can't tell you anything in detail. This is classified information, or mostly, anyway. I can tell you that I was part of a small team who infiltrated deeply and secretly. We were on a mission and deep in enemy territory. Intelligence is often gathered via listening devices, some high-tech, other times just basic radio-frequency stuff. We'd been listening for several hours and I had information," he explained and tapped a finger to his temple. "In here. I was a translator and because of the situation we were in there was no time to document all the intelligence."

She nodded. "And?"

"Radio contact was made. A pickup point was decided. And then the mission turned bad and we were suddenly surrounded by insurgents. There seemed no way out. We were bunkered down behind a ridge of rock and held that position for eight hours, randomly exchanging gunfire. We all knew it was highly unlikely we'd all survive. Decisions had to be made. And then three other soldiers in my unit lost their lives making sure I got back safely. For the greater good, you see," he said cynically. "Funny—but nothing felt good about any of it."

She took a step closer and grabbed his hands. "I'm so sorry."

"Yeah…me, too. Do you get it now? Do you understand why—?"

"I understand guilt," she said, cutting him off gently. "And I understand why you feel as you do. But they were doing their job, right? Just as you were? Which doesn't make it your fault."

"I know that…logically," he said and gripped her hands. "But there's this thing about logic—it has a way of camouflaging truth and grief and guilt. So it doesn't matter how often I tell myself I'm not to blame. It doesn't matter that the intelligence eventually got into the right hands. It doesn't matter that the insurgents were defeated because of that intelligence. Because all that matters is that three lives were lost…three families are mourning… three men are dead…and I'm not."

She sucked in a sharp breath. "Are you saying you wish you had been?"

Brant shook his head. "Of course not. I'm grateful that I survived. I'm glad my family isn't grieving and I'm certainly glad I'm here, in this room, with you."

She shuddered and he pulled her closer. The awareness between them amplified and Brant fought the urge he had to kiss her. He wasn't going to coerce her in any way. They had heat and attraction between them, and he knew it was powerful for them both, but if they went any further it had to be her decision.

"Brant…" Her voice trailed off and then she inhaled sharply.

"Yes, Lucia?"

"I want to be with you… I do. I want it more than anything. I want you to kiss me and make love to me. But I also want everything else that goes with that."

He knew that. He knew what she was looking for. Commitment. Security. A life. Probably marriage down the track. He'd never been one for commitment and didn't see that changing anytime soon.

"Then you decide what you want to do, Lucy," he said and released her gently. "You know who I am. I've told you what happened and even though you might not understand why, it closed off something inside of me. And because of that I won't make you promises I can't keep. But I want you…and that's all I can offer right now."

Brant turned and left the room. He wasn't going to deceive her.

He cared about her too much for that.

By the time Lucy left the Parker ranch it was past ten o'clock. She drove into town with a heavy heart.

I want you...

His words toyed around with her good sense. She should run a mile. She should forget all about him. Instead she pulled up outside the Loose Moose and stared at the big door. She looked up and saw there was a light beaming in the upstairs window. He *was* home. He'd left the wedding around the same time she had, without speaking to her. If she went inside now they would make love…no doubt about it. If she drove on, Lucy sensed she'd never hear from him again.

And that was…unbearable.

Thirty seconds later she was tapping on the door.

When he opened the door he was still dressed in his suit, minus the jacket. He looked so handsome and his dark hair gleamed in the lamplight overhead.

"Hi."

His eyes glittered brilliantly. "Hello."

"Can I come in?"

He stepped aside and she quickly walked over the threshold. The door closed and she turned. He stood excruciatingly still and Lucy's dangling courage disappeared.

"You look really beautiful tonight," he said softly.

"I think you said that already."

He shrugged. "I don't think you really know how beautiful you are…inside and out."

Heat spotted her cheeks as she stripped off her coat

and placed it on a workbench. "I'm not beautiful…not really."

"You are to me," he said and half smiled. "You're also argumentative and a little stubborn and have a bad temper. But you do look really great in that dress." He took a few steps toward her. "I should have danced with you tonight. I wanted to."

Lucy swallowed hard and then grinned. "It was like prom all over again. No date. No dancing."

Brant stared at her, his gaze unwavering. He came closer and grabbed her hand, linking their fingers in a way that felt so intimate, Lucy's entire body grew hotter with each passing second.

"Come with me," he said and led her across the room.

She thought they were going upstairs, to his bedroom, to his bed, and her nerves had her legs shaking. But he walked past the stairwell and toward the back of the tavern. It had once been a pool room but was now filled with several tables and a stage, as well as two new gaming tables. There was a dance floor and jukebox in one corner. Brant didn't release her as he headed for the jukebox and flicked a few switches before it roared into life. He took a moment to choose a song and then turned her toward the dance floor.

Lucy dropped her bag onto one of the tables and went with him into the center of the floor as the music began. Kenny Chesney's voice suddenly filled the room and Lucy curved herself into Brant's embrace. They fit together, she thought as his right arm came around her waist and his other hand cupped her nape. And then they danced. Slowly, closely, as though they'd done it a hundred times before. His hand was warm against her neck and he rubbed her skin softly with his fingertips.

Lucy gripped his shoulders, felt the muscles harden

beneath her palms and moved closer. There was nothing but clothing between them and she could feel the heat of his body connect with hers.

And then he kissed her, deeply, passionately, as if he couldn't get enough of the taste of her mouth.

Lucy kissed him back and heard him groan as his fingers tangled in her hair. She held on to his shoulders and lost herself in his kiss.

When the song ended Lucy pulled back, breathless, knees trembling.

"Take me upstairs," she said softly.

"Are you sure?"

Lucy nodded. Whatever happened, she wanted this part of him. She wanted his touch and his possession and body next to hers. In that moment, nothing else mattered.

It took about a minute to walk upstairs and into his bedroom. The big bed was covered in a functional blue quilt and, other than two narrow side tables, a small chair and a wardrobe, the room was clearly just a place to sleep. He pulled the curtains together, flicked on the bedside lamp and turned off the overhead light. Then he unclipped his watch, placing it on one of the side tables.

Lucy was so nervous she was sure he could hear her knees knocking together. But she didn't move. She only watched him, mesmerized, well aware that he'd certainly done it all before, many times and with many other women. But she didn't want to think about that.

He tugged at his tie, dropped it on the chair and then began to slowly unbutton his shirt.

She absorbed him with her gaze and her palms itched with the urge to rush forward and run her hands over his chest. He was broad and muscular and so effortlessly masculine. Once the shirt disappeared, his hands rested on his belt and she gulped. Of course she'd seen plenty of naked men in her line of work. But this was different. This was Brant. She was going to touch him. Kiss him. Make love with him. And he would do the same with her. She was suddenly filled with a mixture of fear and wonderment.

"Everything all right, Lucy?" Brant asked as he kicked off his shoes.

She swallowed hard. "Yes…everything's fine."

He pulled the belt through the loops and dropped it on the floor. "*Lucia*…come here." She walked across the room and he grasped her hand. "You're shaking. Are you nervous?"

She nodded. "A little."

"Don't be," he said as gently swiveled her around. "We'll just take it slow."

His fingers found the tab of her zipper and he slowly eased it down. His mouth brushed across her shoulder and she moaned, overwhelmed by the sheer longing she felt for his touch. The gown slipped off her shoulders and fell to her feet. She stepped out of it and inhaled as she turned to face him.

"You're so…" He raked his gaze over her, taking in the red-lace bra and matching thong she'd bought on a whim months earlier and was suddenly very glad she'd teamed with the red dress.

Normally, Lucy was self-conscious of her curves. She never dressed overtly sexy and her underwear was usually the sensible nondescript kind. But the desire in his eyes was hot and real and made her skin burn.

She flipped off her heels and stood in front of him. "I can't believe we're here."

"Believe it," he said and tugged her closer. "I've thought of little else for weeks."

His words enflamed her and Lucy abandoned her

nerves and accepted his kiss. They were on the bed seconds later and she was breathless as his hands caressed her from knee to rib cage. His kissed her throat, her shoulders and the curve of her breasts. Her entire body was on fire and her hands clamored to touch him. She felt his heart beat madly in his chest, twirled her fingers on the trail of hair on his belly and heard him suck in a sharp, agonized breath. He was as weak for her touch as she was for his and the knowledge gave her courage. She didn't feel out of her depth. Touching him felt like the most natural thing in the world.

He dispensed with her bra quickly and touched her breasts with his hands and then his mouth. It was delicious, exquisite torture, and she threw her head back as his tongue toyed with one nipple and then the other. He pushed her thong down her hips and for the next half hour he gave but didn't take.

He kissed her, caressed and stroked her skin. He touched her with his hands, his fingertips and his mouth to the point that every inch of body was übersensitive to his touch. She clung to him. She whispered words she'd never imagined she would utter to another soul and experienced such narcotic pleasure than she was quickly a quivering mass of need.

He knew, somehow, that the sensitive skin behind her knee was an erogenous zone and his touch there made her head spin. He knew that trailing his tongue along the underside of her breast would drive her wild. And, finally, when he touched her intimately, she was so aroused she almost bucked off the bed begging for him to give her the release she suddenly craved. As inexperienced as she was, Lucy somehow knew what she wanted.

"Please," she begged and met his mouth hungrily.

"Not yet," he said with a raspy breath as he caressed

her gently. "We have all the time in the world. There's no need to hurry, Lucia."

There was every need. She wanted to feel him above her, around her, inside her.

But he knew what he was doing. There was a gentle rhythm in his magical touch as he continued to stroke her. And then she was gone, caught up in a vortex of pleasure so intense she thought she might pass out. She moaned and said his name, felt her entire body shudder as she came back down to earth. It was beautiful, frightening, overwhelming…and she knew there was more.

When her hands stopped shaking, she fumbled with the button and zipper on his trousers. She heard laughter rumble in his chest at her eagerness and he quickly took over the task. In a second he was naked and above her, chest to breast, his arousal undeniable.

He reached across the bed and grabbed something from the bedside table. When she realized he had a condom in his hand, she blushed wildly.

"Oh… I didn't think about that," she said suddenly self-conscious.

He chuckled. "Now, Doctor, I don't have to tell you how babies are made, do I?"

Lucy's heart did a backflip at the very idea of having his baby. It was one of the things she wanted most in the world.

"Ah…no. Just caught up in the moment, I guess."

He smiled and kissed her. A deep, drugging kiss that had possession stamped all over it. And she didn't mind one bit. She wanted to be his. She longed for it. Right then and all night long. And forever.

He moved over her and Lucy ran her hands eagerly down his back, urging him closer. She closed her eyes and waited. She knew there would be pain, knew her inexperienced body would resist at first. But she wanted him so much, needed him so much, any fear quickly disappeared. He hovered over her, kissing her neck, her jaw, her mouth, and Lucy welcomed him.

He stilled, rested his weights on his arms and stared down into her face. “Everything all right?”

She nodded. “Of course.”

“You’re tense,” he said and kissed her again. “Relax.”

She tried and when he finally was inside her she felt a sharp, stinging pain that made her wince.

He stilled again, more pronounced this time, and his gaze sharpened. “Lucy?” There was query and uncertainty in his voice. And he still didn’t move. “What…are you…have you never—?”

“Brant.” She said his name urgently, cutting off his words. She held on to his shoulders when she felt him withdraw. “No…don’t…please…stay with me.”

He knew.

And for a moment she thought she’d lost him.

His gaze bore into hers, absorbing her, asking the question and getting the answer he clearly hadn’t expected.

“Lucy…” He said her name again, as if he was torn, unsure.

She gripped him hard and pulled him closer. “Don’t leave me.”

He gaze wavered and it seemed to take an eternity for him to relax. But he did, finally. He stayed, and that was all she cared about. She felt complete for the first time in her life. Lucy wrapped her arms around him and urged him toward her intimately. He moved against her, kissing her mouth with a mixture of passion and disbelief. And she drew strength from his mixed emotions. She kissed him back. She touched him. She told him what she wanted.

She matched him. They continued that way, moving together, creating a rhythm that was mind-blowing. And when release came again it got them both. Lucy held on as he shuddered above her, loving him with all her heart as she got lost in a world of pleasure so gloriously intense she could only say his name on a sigh.

When it was over, he moved and rolled onto his back. Lucy stayed where she was, breathless and still mindless from the tiny aftershocks of sensation pulsing over her skin. After a few minutes, Brant got up and disappeared into the bathroom. When he returned Lucy still lay on the bed, a sheet half draped over her hips.

He sat on the end of the bed and his skin dappled golden in the lamplight. Lucy reached out to touch him and he flinched. Then he looked at her. There was no mistaking it. He was angry.

"Brant, I—"

"That was your first time?" he asked quietly.

She nodded. "Yes, but—"

"Goddamn it, Lucy! You should have told me."

"It doesn't—"

"Whatever you're going to say," he said, cutting her off as he got to his feet and pulled on a pair of jeans that were on the chair. "Just save it. Because if you think it doesn't matter, you're wrong. It matters, Lucy. It matters so damn much."

He walked out of the room and she heard his feet thump on every stair. Once he was downstairs she stretched and sighed. Her body was still humming, still remembering every touch. She'd imagined making love with Brant countless times and being with him had exceeded anything she'd imagined. She had never expected to feel such a deep, fulfilling connection to another person. If she'd ever doubted that she was in love with him, those doubts were now well and truly gone.

Lucy sat up and swung her knees over the edge of the bed. He was angry and, in typical Brant fashion, when he was mad he closed down. And since Lucy preferred to face an issue head-on, she knew they had to talk.

She got up, grabbed the shirt he'd discarded and slipped her arms into the sleeves. It felt warm against her skin and the scent of his cologne clung to the fabric. She made a bathroom stop. She was still a little tender, but he'd been so gentle with her she knew it would pass quickly. Then she took a deep breath and headed downstairs.

Brant rarely drank hard liquor anymore. But he downed a second belt of bourbon and let the heat slide down his throat.

He was wound up. He couldn't sit still. He paced the rooms downstairs and tried to work out what he was feeling. Guilt. Confusion. Disbelief.

I should have known.

The words kept chanting in his head.

There had always been something innocent about Lucy Monero. She was an intriguing mix of confidence and coyness. Her kisses were sweet and making love to her had been like nothing he'd felt before. Her touch hadn't been tentative, but exploring, inquisitive...like she was experiencing something new and exciting. Of course, now he knew why.

A virgin.

He could barely believe it. Okay, so she *was* kind of wholesome. But she was also twenty-seven. And a successful doctor who'd gone to college and medical school and had lived a full life. Never in his wildest dreams would he have imagined she would be untouched.

"Brant?"

He looked up. She stood silhouetted in the doorway. She was wearing his shirt and with the light behind he could make out every curve and dip of her naked body beneath. His libido spiked instantly. Her hair was mussed and loose around her shoulders and he couldn't help but remember how he'd fisted a handful of her beautiful locks and kissed her throat and neck and breasts. He'd wanted her as he'd never wanted anyone before. Damn…he still wanted her. Everything about her was pure invitation… her skin, her lips, her curves. She was so lovely. So sweet. And sexy, too, even though he was pretty sure she didn't know it.

Brant shook off his thoughts and sat on the edge of one of the tables. He knew they needed to talk. But first he had to ensure she was all right. "Are you okay?"

"I'm fine." She stepped closer and the light behind turned the shirt translucent. "Are *you* okay?"

He shook his head. "We need to talk about this, Lucy."

She bit her bottom lip. "I know you're angry and—"

"I'm not angry," he said. "I'm a little confused. Frankly, I don't understand why you didn't tell me."

She shrugged. "Well, it's not the kind of thing that generally comes up in conversation."

"You're twenty-seven years old," he said flatly. "And up until half an hour ago, you were a virgin. I think that warrants some kind of conversation, don't you?"

She took a few more steps. "Okay… I probably should have said something."

"Probably?"

"All right," she said on a sharp breath. "I just didn't want to make a big deal out of it."

"It *is* a big deal, Lucy," he said quietly. "And if you've waited this long, you know that."

She sat on a chair by one of the pool tables. "I just wanted to be with you tonight."

Brant pushed himself off the table and dragged a chair beside her. "I wanted to be with you, too," he said as he sat. "But it was your first time, Lucy…and that should mean something."

"It did," she whispered. "At least, it did to me."

Guilt hit him squarely between the shoulder blades. "Look, of course it was…great. You're beautiful and sexy…and it's obvious I'm attracted to you."

She raised her hands. "But that's all it is, right?"

"I haven't deliberately misled you, Lucy," he said soberly. "I try not to mislead anyone."

"You're not serious?"

"What does that mean?"

"It means," she said quietly, "that for the past couple of weeks you've been courting me and haven't even realized it."

His back stiffened. "That's not true. I only—"

"Pizza and a football game?" she reminded him. "Comforting me when I had a bad day at work? An impromptu Thanksgiving dinner? Text messages? Phone calls saying how much you missed me? Really…what did you think you were doing?"

He stilled. Was she right? Was he so blind? He liked her…a lot. But the idea of it being more than that made his head ache.

"I guess… I guess I *wasn't* thinking," he admitted. He took one of her hands in his. "Did I hurt you? The first time can be—"

"You didn't hurt me," she said and pulled her hand away. "And you're working yourself up about it for some reason of your own. I made a decision tonight, Brant... and I made that decision because I *am* twenty-seven years old and know exactly what I want." She got to her feet. "Yes, I have not had a lover before tonight. And maybe I didn't tell you that exactly, but I've told you plenty about my life and the kind of person I am. I was a geek in high school, *remember*?" she said with emphasis. "I was a bookworm. I didn't have boyfriends. I didn't have a date for the prom. And I told you I didn't date in college. What did you think that meant? That I was amusing myself with one-night stands instead?"

"Of course not," he said quickly. "I only—"

"I didn't deliberately set out to be a virgin at twenty-seven. And even if I did, I'm sure that doesn't quite make me a candidate for *Guinness World Records*."

"That's not what I meant to—"

"I was grieving my mom," she said hotly. "I was still coming to terms with the accident. And the truth is, I was so *messed up*, I didn't want to get involved with anyone. And then when my roommate was attacked it shut something off inside me and all I wanted to do was become a good doctor. That's all I concentrated on. That's all I wanted. Not a date. Not a boyfriend. Not sex."

She was breathing so hard her chest rose up and down and Brant was instantly aroused. She walked away, hands on hips, clearly irritated. He stood and followed her around the pool table.

"But you want that now?" he asked. "A boyfriend? Sex?"

She stopped walking and turned, glaring at him. "You'd make a rotten boyfriend."

He couldn't help grinning. Even when she was madder than hell she was beautiful.

"You're right about that."

She looked at his chest and then her gaze rose to meet his eyes. "So, I should probably leave."

"If that's what you want."

She scowled and still looked beautiful. "You'd let me go so easily?"

"I never said it would be easy."

She seemed to sway closer. "None of this is easy, is it? Feeling. Wanting. Maybe…" she said as a hand came up and touched his chest. "Maybe it's not meant to be easy. Maybe the struggle is what makes it worthwhile."

"Maybe," he agreed and placed his hand over hers.

"So," she said softly. "What do we do now?"

Brant clasped his hands to her hips and lifted her onto the edge of the pool table. "Now," he said as he settled between her thighs and wound his arms around her, "I guess we do this."

She sighed, all resistance disappearing. "For how long?"

"For now. For as long as it lasts," he said and kissed her.

He knew that Lucy was thinking forever.

And that was something Brant didn't believe in.

Chapter Eleven

Lucy didn't want to think…or imagine…that six days into their *thing* she actually had a boyfriend. But Friday night, after they'd spent two hours in bed together and were now in her kitchen, eating enchiladas and drinking coffee, she figured she could call it a *relationship.* Of sorts.

When they were together Brant was attentive and charming and certainly seemed unable to get enough of her. They made love a lot. He arrived at her place every afternoon at five thirty and was always gone by midnight. They ate dinner, watched television, talked about mundane things and regularly had hot, uninhibited sex that turned her sensible brain to mush. But he never slept over and always called her the following morning to see how she was.

She was on day shift at the hospital and got to sleep in until eight every morning to combat the fatigue she felt, which meant a mad rush getting showered and dressed and to work on time. But she didn't care. She was wrapped in a lovely kind of bubble that had everything to do with the fact that she was crazy in love with Brant and adored every moment they spent together.

"I have the weekend off," she said and sipped her coffee.

Brant looked at her over the mug in his hands. "I know."

She half smiled. "Did you want to do something tomorrow? Or Sunday?"

"I have the kitchen going in at the tavern this weekend," he said quietly. "And the new chef is arriving tomorrow, so I'll be tied up both days. Plus, I want to try and see Uncle Joe. I'll let you know, okay?"

"Oh...sure."

He drank his coffee and then stood, collecting their plates. "There's a game on if you're interested?"

Football? She was learning to like the game and if it meant cuddling up on the couch with Brant, all the better. She nodded. "I was thinking, if you're coming over tomorrow why don't you stay the night and we could go into town Sunday morning for breakfast?"

He stilled and stared at her. "We'll see."

Code for "no chance." Right. Lucy wondered if he was worried about being seen with her. It was a small town and people talked. Although, since his truck had been parked outside her house every night for close to a week, she figured they had probably been outed already. Of course, Kayla had called every day, and Brooke and Ash, who were a little more discreet, had been texting her off and on for two days. Colleen had been noticeably absent and Lucy figured the woman was giving them space.

"If you don't want to spend the night, just say so."

His gaze sharpened. "That's not what I said."

She shrugged. "Actions speak louder than words."

She immediately saw the gleam in his eyes. "They certainly do."

Lucy smiled, caught her bottom lip between her teeth and felt a familiar surge of desire pulse through her body. "Prove it," she said and got up and raced into the living room, well aware he would be ten paces behind her.

By the time he caught up she was turned on and ready for him. He hauled her into his arms and kissed her hotly. She kissed him back and wrapped her arms around his waist. They made it to the sofa in three seconds flat and began stripping clothes off in their usual hurry. She straddled him and linked her arms around his neck.

"Contraception," he said raggedly.

Lucy dug into the pocket of her robe, extracted a foil packet and then rattled it between her fingertips. "Voilà!"

He smiled against her mouth and kissed her hotly. "Sweetheart, you never cease to amaze me."

Lucy's heart surged. It was thc first endearment he'd ever called her and she liked it more than she'd imagined. They made love quickly, passionately, as if they couldn't get enough of one another. It was hot and erotic and mind-blowing. Afterward, Brant grabbed the blanket from the back of the sofa and wrapped it around her shoulders.

"It's cold in here. I've let the fire burn down too low," he said and hooked a thumb in the direction of the fireplace. "Remind me to stock up your firewood next week."

His consideration warmed her heart. He was caring and kind and she loved him. And had almost told him so a dozen times in the past week. But she always held back. He wasn't ready for any kind of declaration.

Lucy nuzzled his neck and pressed herself against his chest. "Thank you."

They watched the football game, fooled around a little on the sofa and by eleven-thirty he bailed. She gave him a lingering kiss in the doorway and watched through the front window as he drove away. As usual, once he'd gone, Lucy experienced a kind of aching loneliness. She knew it was foolish. Knew that whatever she was feeling, Brant was certainly not on the same page. He liked her. He wanted her. But that was all he was good for. She'd tried getting him to talk more about what had happened in Afghanistan, but he would shut her down every time she broached the subject. She knew he'd been to see Dr. Allenby again, but had no idea if he was making any progress or if he'd made another appointment. Despite how close they'd become, there was a restless kind of energy around him that was impossible to ignore. It had her on edge…and waiting for the inevitable fallout.

Strangely, he didn't text her Saturday morning and by ten o'clock she gave in and sent him a message. He replied about half an hour later, saying he was tied up and would speak to her later. It left her with a heavy, uneasy feeling in her heart.

Kayla and Brooke dropped in to see her at lunchtime, carrying a pizza and a six pack of pear cider.

"It's about time you came up for air," Kayla said with a grin as they all headed for the kitchen. "By the flushed expression, I take it everything is going well?"

Lucy shrugged. She wasn't sure she wanted to have a post mortem about her relationship with Brant. It felt… disloyal. That was stupid, of course, because Kayla and Brooke were her closest friends and she could always rely on their support and understanding. But she'd essentially always been a private person, and being with Brant on the most intimate level was not something she wanted to discuss or dissect.

"Yeah…fine," she said and grabbed plates from the cupboard. "How are you both?"

Brooke, certainly the most diplomatic of the pair, gave her arm a gentle squeeze when they all sat. "We're worried about you, that's all."

"I'm fine," she assured them. "I promise."

Kayla's perfectly beautiful face was marred with a frown. "We don't quite believe you. And we're here if you need to talk."

She knew that. But, strangely, the only person she wanted to confide in was Brant. She liked the way he listened. She liked the way he stroked her hair when she'd talked about her mom and the accident and how helpless she'd felt. She liked how there was no judgment, no condescending advice…only his deep voice assuring her the pain and hurt would eventually pass. The irony was, it was exactly what she wanted to say to him. They were both broken in their own way. Sure, she'd moved on and seen a therapist and didn't have bad dreams anymore, but a part of her would always grieve for the years she'd lost with her parents. And Brant understood that grief better than anyone ever had.

Sometimes when he'd dozed a little after they'd made love, she'd witnessed his restlessness. He had bad dreams, she was sure of it. She hadn't said anything to him about it, but knew he was certainly reliving the horror of what he'd seen in the war. And it broke her heart that she couldn't help him through his pain.

She looked at her friends and felt their sympathetic stares through to her bones.

"I'm fine, like I said. It's early days, that's all."

"Good," Kayla said and sighed heavily. "We just weren't sure if you knew about the woman he was with this morning."

Her back stiffened. "What woman?"

"I saw him at the coffee place next door to O'Sullivan's. They were talking. It looked serious."

He was with another woman. And it looked serious.

Lucy wondered if there had ever been a bigger fool than her. But she pasted on a smile and shrugged. "I'm sure there's a perfectly reasonable explanation."

Her friends didn't look too convinced. Heat burned the backs of her eyes and tears threatened to spill.

"I'm in love with Brant," she said honestly.

Brooke patted her arm again. "Yeah, we know that."

"I've never been in love before," she admitted, aware her friends knew it already.

Brooke offered a gentle smile. "Does he love you back?"

Lucy shook her head, suddenly hurting all over. "I don't think he believes he's capable of loving anyone."

And knowing he believed he was that hollow inside made her heart ache.

Saturday lunch at his mother's wasn't generally a chore, but Brant was in no mood to be put under the microscope by his parent or his brother. He planned to stop in for an hour before he got back to the tavern to tackle the painting. He'd had half the kitchen installed at the tavern that morning and the contractors were coming back the following day to finish the job. He'd also interviewed the new chef and discovered the thirtysomething single mom had excellent credentials and stellar references. She also had nowhere to live, since she was relocating from Montana with her young son, and Brant had assured her he would help her find suitable accommodation. His apartment above the tavern would do the job, and since he hadn't planned on making it his permanent residence, he needed to think about getting a real home of his own. A house, with a yard and a porch and a maybe a swing set out back.

As soon as he had the thought, Brant shook himself. He had no place in his life for yards and swing sets. That was the kind of life his brother had. Not him.

Only…he kept thinking about it. About yards and swing sets and Lucy Monero.

"Everything okay?"

His brother's voice jerked him into the present. Grady and Marissa had forgone a honeymoon and instead planned to head to Nevada with her father, Rex, after Christmas to meet her newly discovered extended family. Brant hadn't been home for the holidays in six years and suspected this one was going to be filled with the usual family gatherings and gift-giving.

"Fine," he said and met his brother's gaze for a moment. They were in the living room, watching a game on television. "How's married life?"

"Amazing." Grady grinned. "You should try it for yourself."

He wasn't about to admit that he'd thought about it many times over the past week. About as often as he'd thought about *ending* his relationship with Lucy. Damn… he didn't want to think of it in terms of being a *relationship*, but how could he not? She'd gifted him the most intimate part of herself and the responsibility of that gift was wreaking havoc with his integrity and moral compass. Lucy wasn't a casual kind of woman. Lucy Monero was the *marrying* kind. If he kept seeing her that's where they'd end up. He was sure of it. And he couldn't. He wouldn't. Having sex with her was addling his brain. He felt weak. Out of control.

He stared at the television and spoke. "I've done something really stupid."

Grady glanced sideways. "And what's that?"

"Lucy."

His brother chuckled softly. "Yeah, I heard. Mom's over the moon. But you know it might just turn out to be the smartest thing you've ever done."

He shook his head. "I can't give her what she wants."

"What's that?"

"Everything," he replied.

"And why do you think you can't give it to her?" Grady asked, more serious.

He exhaled heavily. "Because I'm not made that way. I don't know…maybe I was once. But…"

"The war changed you?" Grady said. "No surprise there. It would change anyone."

Brant nodded. "I've been talking to Dr. Allenby…you know, at the veterans home."

"How's it going?"

He shrugged. "He knows his stuff. He's easy to talk to and doesn't push too hard. But I've talked to army shrinks before and it hasn't made any difference. What's in here—" he put a finger to his temple "—is there forever. I can't escape it. I can't deny it. I'm just trying to camouflage it so I can lead a normal sort of life."

"And Lucy?" Grady prompted.

"She rips through that camouflage without even knowing it." He ran a frustrated hand through his hair. "Or maybe she does. I don't know. All I do know is that when I'm around her I feel… I feel so damned…"

"Vulnerable?" his brother said and sighed. "I hate to break this to you, but that's got nothing to do with you being changed somehow by what you experienced in the war."

Brant frowned. "Then what is it?"

"It's because you're in love with her," Grady said frankly.

Every part of him stilled and he quickly dismissed his brother's words. "I'm not. I just feel…responsible."

Grady's eyes widened. "For what? She's not pregnant is she?"

Brant scowled quickly, looking around to make sure his mother or sister-in-law weren't nearby and spoke quietly. "No. But she…" His words trailed off. He wasn't about to betray Lucy's confidence, as much as he felt like spilling his woes to his brother. "It's private and not up for discussion. But let's just say that she…surprised me."

His brother shook his head. "You can be cryptic if you have to, but the truth is you've always had blinders on when it came to Lucy Monero. She was the girl next door, remember? The girl who used to look at you with puppy-dog eyes and who you never noticed because you were too busy trying to score with Trudy What's-Her-Name. Now you've come to come to your senses and finally noticed her and it turns out she still has a thing for you." Grady's eyes gleamed. "Sounds like love to me."

Brant shook his head. "You can make fun all you like, but I have my reasons for feeling responsible for hurting her. You're right, she waited for me," he said, flinching inwardly, wondering what Grady would think if he knew the true meaning of the words. "She chose me and I have no idea why. All week I've been trying to work out ways to end it. But then she looks at me, or touches me, and I'm done for. I feel as though I'm in a corner and there's no way out. And the thing is," he admitted wearily, "part of me doesn't want a way out."

Grady smiled and slapped him on the shoulder. "Well, I guess there's only one thing you can do."

"What's that?"

"You should do the smart thing and marry her."

When Lucy didn't hear from Brant again on Saturday, or on Sunday morning, she began imagining a dozen different scenarios. Maybe his coffee date had turned into something else. Something more. But by midday she'd worked herself up and was so mad with him she knew if she stayed home she'd stew all day and ruin what was left of her weekend.

She drove to Kayla's in the afternoon and ended up staying for dinner. Kayla was all commiseration and support and by the time they'd consumed three cups of coffee and a packet of Oreos, Lucy had convinced herself that Brant was seeing someone else and his silence meant he was breaking things off between them. She left at eight o'clock and drove down the street, pulling over beneath a streetlight. She grabbed her cell and sent him a text.

I need to see you.

A couple of minutes later she got a reply.

I'm kinda busy right now. But I'll call you later.

Later? Right. Her rage turned to hurt and then her hurt morphed back into rage. Well, if he was seeing someone else she certainly wanted to know about it. She might be foolishly naive...but she wasn't going to be a naive fool!

I'll be there in five minutes.

She didn't wait for a response and drove back into town. Six minutes later she pulled up outside the tavern.

Lucy didn't bother with her coat, instead she grabbed her tote, got out of the car, marched up to the door and banged so hard her knuckles hurt. The big door swung back and he stood in the doorway, dressed in old jeans that rode low on his hips, a long-sleeved, pale gray Henley T-shirt and sneakers.

He was also covered in paint from head to toe.

"What are you doing?" she asked.

"Painting myself," he said, grabbing her arm and hauling her across the threshold. "More the point, what are you doing out this late and without a coat? Are you trying to catch pneumonia?"

She shivered as the cold from the air outside seeped through her thin clothing. "My coat is in the car."

"There's a fire going in the back room," he said. "Warm yourself up while I grab you a sweater."

Lucy walked to the rear of the tavern and stood by the big fireplace. She noticed a couple of ladders with a timber plank between them and a tin of paint on its side and a pool of paint on the floor. He returned a couple of minutes later with a blue zip-up sweater. She took it and placed her arms through the sleeves.

"Um, it looks like you had a little accident?" She pointed to the paint spill.

"Someone texted me," he replied pointedly. "I was on the ladder with a bucket of paint in one hand and brush in another. I went for my phone, it slipped out of my hand and almost landed in the paint. I figured a tin of spilled paint was the lesser of two evils."

Lucy bit back a grin. He still had some explaining to do. "Are you seeing someone else?"

"What?" he shot back as he grabbed a towel from the bench top and wiped at some of the paint on his face and neck.

Lucy stepped forward and took the towel from him. "Someone else," she said again as she removed a smear of paint from his jaw. "As in, the woman you had coffee with yesterday."

He sighed, clearly exasperated. "Faith O'Halloran has just moved to Cedar River from Montana with her young son," he explained. "She's the new chef. The coffee *date* was an interview."

Lucy fought the sudden embarrassment clinging to her skin. Damn Kayla and her overly suspicious mind. "Oh… I see."

He took the towel back. "So, is the interrogation over?"

She shrugged lightly. "Mostly. You've got paint in your hair." She grabbed the towel again and started on the paint smear on his throat. "And everywhere else, by the look of things. Why are you working so late anyhow?"

"I've got some of the interior fit-out next week," he said, standing perfectly still. "I told you I was working this weekend."

She avoided his gaze and kept wiping his throat. "You said you were busy."

"Yes, busy…working." He shook his head. "The kitchen went in this weekend, remember?" He took the towel and tossed it aside. "I'm going to clean up this mess, take a shower and then we're going to talk. Or—" He grabbed her around the waist, careful not to get paint on her clothes, and looked down into her upturned face. "You could take a shower with me and we could skip the talking for an hour or two."

Lucy liked the sound of that idea.

An hour later they were lying side by side on his bed, spent and breathing hard.

"Incidentally," Brant said as he entwined their fingers. "I'm trying not to take offense at the fact you thought I was seeing someone else. I'm many things, Lucia, but unfaithful is not one of them."

Lucy grimaced. "I'm sorry. Put it down to inexperience. I'm not very knowledgeable when it comes to this kind of…" She waggled the fingers on her other hand. "Thing."

"You're not alone," he said quietly. "I haven't exactly embraced commitment for the past decade."

She grinned. "Your virgin heart. My virgin body. That's quite a combination."

He laughed softly and his grip tightened. "Lucy… I'd like to know something."

"Sure. What?"

"I don't quite know how to put this without sounding incredibly egotistical…but why did you really wait so long to have a physical relationship with someone? Did it have anything to do with me? Or to some old infatuation you may have had from when we were kids?"

Lucy shrugged lightly. "Not consciously. I mean, sure… I did have a little crush on you in high school. But I was so quiet and ridiculously self-conscious in high school. And once I got to college, sex seemed like some kind of tradable commodity. The bed hopping wasn't something I wanted for myself. And then when my roommate was attacked…it just seemed like one complication I didn't need."

"But once you were working and out of college, surely there were men interested in you?"

"Not so much," she admitted. "I think that when a person puts a wall up for long enough, people stop trying to find a way over the top. And I had a wall that was ten feet high."

"What about Kieran O'Sullivan?" he asked.

"A friend," she replied. "No blip, remember?"

"So...there was no one else you were interested in being with? Ever?"

Heat crawled over her skin. How did she respond without sounding like an immature, love-struck fool? "I guess I didn't want to kiss a whole lot of frogs before I discovered princes didn't really exist."

Silence enveloped the dimly lit room for a moment. Lucy could hear him breathing and watched the steady rise and fall of his chest. After a moment he spoke again.

"Are you saying you hadn't..." His tone took on a kind of wary disbelief. "That you hadn't—"

"That I hadn't really kissed anyone before you?" she finished for him. "I guess I hadn't."

She heard his sharp intake of breath and felt the tension seep through his body. "Lucy...why me?"

Heat caught in her throat and she swallowed hard. "You know why."

He sighed heavily. "You could have any man you wanted...someone who can give you what you're looking for...marriage...family..."

When his words trailed off, Lucy's heart twisted. "And that's not you, is that what you're saying?"

He sighed again, wearily, as though he had a great burden pressing down on his chest. "A week ago you said I'd been courting you and didn't even know it...and you were right. That was unfair of me. I don't—"

"Am I being dumped?" she asked hotly, jackknifing up.

He straightened. "That's not what I meant."

"Then what?" she demanded. "Your hot-and-cold routine is tiring, Brant." Lucy shook her head and sighed. "How about we get some sleep and talk about this tomorrow?"

Brant stood, unselfconsciously naked and so gorgeous

she almost crawled across the bed and pressed herself against him. But his next words turned her inside out.

"You can't stay here."

She watched as he grabbed a pair of fresh jeans from the wardrobe and slipped them on.

Lucy scrambled her legs together. "Now you're kicking me out?"

He ran a hand through his hair. "I just think it would be best if you went home."

Lucy got to her feet and stood toe-to-toe with him. His gaze raked over her, hot and filled with an almost reluctant desire. Even when they were in the middle of a crisis, the attraction they had for one another was undeniable.

Lucy stood her ground. "No."

His gaze narrowed. "No?"

"I'm staying."

He inhaled sharply and grabbed her dress from the chair in the corner. "Get dressed."

"Forget it, soldier," she said, hands on hips. "Because if I go, I go for good."

"Then go," he said coldly and walked toward the door.

"What is it, Brant?" she demanded as she quickly got into her dress and smoothed the fabric over her hips. "What is it you're so afraid of?"

He stopped instantly and turned. "Afraid?" he echoed, his blue eyes glittering. "I'm not afraid of anything."

"I don't believe you," she snapped, going for his emotional jugular because if she didn't she knew she would lose him forever. "So, what is it? Are you scared that if I spend the night, if I sleep in your bed, that at some point I'm going to witness the *real* you? The you who paces the floorboards at night? The you who breaks out in a cold sweat at two o'clock in the morning? The you who has bad dreams and cries in his sleep?"

He paled instantly. "How…how do you know that?" he asked raggedly.

Her heart ached for him and she pressed a hand to his chest. "Because I *know* you. In here. I'm connected to you in a way I've never been connected to anyone in my life. Don't you get it, Brant? *I love you.*"

It was out.

There was nothing for either of them to hide behind.

Just her heart on the line.

Lucy stared at him, absorbing every feature, every conflicting emotion, evident in his expression. But he didn't speak. He didn't move. He simply looked at her. Into her. Through her. Time seemed to stretch like brittle elastic until, finally, he spoke.

"It's late. Get some sleep."

He turned and left the room and Lucy didn't take a breath until she couldn't hear his footsteps on the stairs. She sat on the bed and sucked in an agonizing breath. Did the man have ice water in his veins? Had she given herself and her love to someone who was impervious to deep feeling?

No...

She knew him. He was kind and compassionate and capable of much more than he realized.

Lucy lay on the bed and closed her eyes. She was so tired, weary from tension and knowing she had to go to work the following day. She inhaled, relaxed her aching shoulders and tried to rest, hopeful that at some point Brant would join her in the big bed.

But he didn't.

Lucy woke up around six and, after a quick bathroom stop, headed downstairs. Brant was awake and behind the main bar, sorting through paint swatches. He wore jeans and a dark sweater and looked so gorgeous her mouth turned dry.

"Hi," she said as cheerfully as she could muster. "Did you manage to get some sleep?"

He hooked a thumb in the direction of a narrow cot in one corner. "A little. You?"

She nodded. "I could make breakfast if you—"

"No...but thank you."

She inhaled sharply. "I guess I should go. I'll just get my things."

Lucy didn't wait for a reply and swiveled on her feet. When she came back downstairs a few minutes later he was near the front of the tavern, piling cut pieces of timber into stacks. "Will I see you later?"

He looked up and straightened. "I'll probably be tied up here all day."

Lucy nodded and walked toward the door. She grabbed the handle, lingered and then turned back to him. "You know, Brant, I've pretty much been in love with you since I was fifteen years old."

He stilled instantly, his blue-eyed gaze riveting her to the spot. The silence between them was suddenly deafening. But she kept going, too far in to back down.

"Do you remember the day you took Trudy to the prom?" she asked but didn't wait for him to respond. "I was at your ranch with my mom. Your dad and Grady were helping my mother sell our ranch and they were all in the kitchen talking and I was sitting by the counter, my head in a book, as always. I used to hang around your ranch and watch you and your brother break and train the horses. Or your mom would give me baking lessons. But that day you came into the room dressed in your suit with a corsage for Trudy and you looked so handsome and grown-up. I knew once school was over that you would be leaving for the military and for the hundredth time I wished I was older, prettier, more popular… And I wished that the corsage was for me and you were taking me to prom."

She sighed, remembering the ache in her young heart that day. "Then you left town and I finished high school and went to college and med school. Years passed and occasionally our paths would cross and you would usually ignore me, and I got used to that. When I returned to town permanently I knew I wanted to work at the hospital and settle down in Cedar River and hopefully find someone to share my life with." Her voice quivered as tears filled her eyes. "Then you came back and I tried to act like I was indifferent and over my silly infatuation. But I knew I'd been fooling myself. Because," she said, putting her hand to her chest as tears fell down her cheeks, "in here…in here I was still that insecure fifteen-year-old girl, dreaming about corsages and going to the prom with Brant Parker."

She pulled her tote close to her body and grabbed the door handle. "I know you believe you can't make a commitment, Brant…and I think I understand why. But, despite how much I love you and love being with you, I need to end this now… I need to stop kidding myself into thinking that what we have is enough for me. Because it's not."

She left the tavern and walked to her car. There was a light blanket of snow on her windshield and she flicked it off before she climbed into the car and drove home.

But the time she arrived at work an hour later, she was hurting all over.

Brant didn't call her that day. Or the next.

However, Lucy called him late Wednesday afternoon and left three messages on his cell.

Because at one o'clock on Wednesday, Joe Parker had another heart attack and was rushed into the ER by the paramedics, but tragically died forty minutes later.

Chapter Twelve

Brant ignored every message on his phone for several days. His uncle was dead and Lucy had left him. She had her reasons and it was probably the right thing. But by Friday he was so wound up he could barely stand being in his own skin.

He met Grady at the funeral home late in the afternoon and finalized the funeral arrangements for the following Monday. The service was to be held at the small cemetery on the edge of town and his uncle would be laid to rest next to their father and grandparents.

"Are you coming back to the ranch?" Grady asked once they'd left the funeral home. "The girls would love to see you."

Brant shook his head. "I've got things to do."

Grady grabbed his shoulder, looked concerned and didn't bother to disguise it. "I don't think you should be alone."

"I'm fine."

When they got to the parking lot, his brother scowled when he saw the motorbike. "Really? In this weather?"

"It was clear when I left the tavern."

Grady held out his palm and caught a few flakes of snow that were now falling. "It's not clear now. I'll drive you back and you can pick the bike up tomorrow."

They both knew he would never leave his motorbike unattended. "Stop fussing like an old woman."

Grady made an exasperated sound. "All right, just be careful riding home in this."

"I will," Brant promised.

His brother nodded and then spoke. "So, have you seen Lucy?"

"No," he replied.

Grady pulled his coat collar up around his neck. "She was there, you know, at the end, holding his hand, giving him comfort."

Brant ignored the tightness in his chest. Yeah, she was good at holding hands. Good at comfort. And good at ending things. "I gotta run. See you tomorrow."

He grabbed his helmet, straddled the bike and was about to say goodbye when his brother spoke again.

"I've always tried to avoid telling you how to live your life or give advice. But I'm going to give you some now. You need to face this, Brant."

His back tensed. "Face what?"

Grady waved a hand. "This thing with Lucy. You served three tours in the military and much of that time was spent on the front line. You're a soldier and one of the bravest men I know. So tell me, what is it about loving this woman that scares you so much?"

"I don't love her," he said coldly as he kicked the bike into life and drove off.

Twenty minutes later, after circling Lucy's block for the third time, he pulled up in her driveway and killed the engine. She wasn't home. He checked his watch. Five-fifteen. She was probably out with her friends at O'Sullivan's. Or she was working. Or on a date.

Brant climbed off the bike and headed for the small porch. He zipped up his leather jacket and sat in the love seat. And waited.

She arrived home twenty minutes later. Wrapped up in a scarlet woolen coat with fake fur trim, black boots, knitted gloves and a white beanie, she looked like she belonged on a Christmas card. Her cheeks were spotted with color and her lips looked lush and red. And imminently kissable.

She seemed neither surprised nor unsurprised to see him as she sat wordlessly beside him on the love seat. He didn't touch her. He didn't dare, despite how much he longed to.

"You didn't reply to my text messages," she said quietly.

"I haven't been doing much of anything this week."

She nodded fractionally. "I was worried about you."

He knew she would have been. "I'm sorry. I've been keeping to myself…trying to make sense of it all."

"And did you?" she asked softly.

He half shrugged. "Not so much. I miss him already."

"I know," she said, her gentle voice somehow soothing some of the pain he felt. "Are you still seeing Dr. Allenby?"

One thing he could always rely on—Lucy Monero never pulled punches or talked in riddles. She was honest and forthright and demanded the same in return.

"Yes," he replied. "I saw him Monday and I have another appointment next week."

"It's helping?"

"I think so…yes."

"I'm glad," she replied and, after a small silence, spoke again. "But what are you really doing here?"

"Grady told me that you were with my uncle when he died," he said, conscious of the heavy weight pressing down on his shoulders. "I just wanted to thank you for that and for your kindness toward him these past few weeks. It's meant a lot to us." He paused, took a breath, felt an uneasy ache in the middle of his chest. "And to me."

She nodded. "I wish I could have done more."

"If yours was the last face he saw before he passed away," Brant said quietly, "then I'm sure he would have died with peace in his heart. So, thank you."

"He was a nice man and I cared about him a great deal." She met his gaze, unwavering. "But anything I did…I did for you."

The sensation in his chest amplified and he swallowed hard. God, she undid him with just a few words. He got up and grabbed the helmet. "I know that. Goodbye, Lucy."

She was frowning. "Should you be biking in this weather?"

Brant looked at the snow still coming down. "I'll be careful."

He got to the steps and then turned. She was still sitting, still looking lost and lovely. His heart thundered in his chest. "You know, I did hear you the other night. Everything you said…you were right to say it. The thing is, I came back to Cedar River to try and forget what happened in Afghanistan. But most days, I still feel as though I'm back on that ridge, back dodging bullets and back hearing the screams of men who died so I could live.

And knowing the only reason it turned out that way is because I had an aptitude for learning another language. If I'd been good at math instead, things would have turned out very different. So, when it's two in the morning and I can't do anything other than stare at the ceiling instead of sleeping, or when my dreams are so bad I wake myself up screaming, I think about how a high school French class probably saved my life."

She stared at him. Through him. Into the very depths of his blood and bones and then further still, right into his soul. No one else had ever done that. No one ever would.

When she spoke again he could barely stand to hear the words. "Part of me wants to wish you and your guilt a long and happy life together. But I can't…because that would simply be my broken heart talking." She got to her feet. "I'll see you at the service on Monday."

Brant looked at her and every conflicting emotion he had banged around in his head. Part of him longed to take her in his arms, part of him ached for her touch. "Thanks again…for everything."

She nodded. "Sure. Goodbye."

Brant watched as she turned, walked into the house and closed the door. Lights flicked on and her silhouette passed by the window, and he was suddenly overwhelmed by an inexplicable urge to knock on her door to beg her to let him stay the night. But then she'd witness his truth—the insomnia, the pacing at two o'clock in the morning, the dampness on his face when he jackknifed out of bed in the middle of a nightmare. He'd tried medication and all it did was dull his senses. Alcohol left him hung over and weary for days. The only solution was to ride through it in private. No one needed to witness his anxiety. She already thought he needed a shrink. If she saw him at two in the morning, drenched in sweat, shaking from fear, she'd run a mile. Or worse, she'd stay. Out of pity and concern. And *that* was worse than not being with her.

It was better this way. For them both.

Brant got through the weekend by working at the tavern and on Monday ran on autopilot during his uncle's funeral. About eighty people turned up for the service, half of them Joe Parker's former army buddies. The minister gave a short reading, as did Grady and then Brant, and while most of the military crew went to Rusty's afterward to celebrate their fallen colleague with a round of beer and shared tales from the war, Brant returned to the ranch with his mother and brother and about twenty close friends, including Lucy.

By the afternoon there were just half a dozen people left, most bailing before the snow came down heavier. Brant sat on the wide veranda, an untouched coffee in his hand. Grady and Brooke were in the kitchen and Marissa was in the playroom with the kids. He spotted Lucy walking across the yard toward the stables. She had on her red coat and it was a stark contrast against the white backdrop of snow. He watched her as she walked, like a vision in red, like a beacon for his weary soul.

A surge of feeling suddenly rose up and hit him squarely in the solar plexus and he couldn't quite get enough air into his lungs. He didn't know what to make of it. Or what to think. Only Lucy could do that. No one had ever had such a profound effect on his peace of mind. His body. His heart.

They'd barely spoken all day. Strangely, it was as though they didn't need to. But during the service he'd felt her behind him and then her small hand had rested on his back. It was all he'd needed to get through the moment. And she'd known that, wordlessly. Because she knew him better than anyone.

He watched her as she walked around alone, moving in circles, almost as though she was so deep in thought she didn't care where she ended up.

"Do you remember what I said to you a few weeks back?"

His mother's voice made him turn his head for a moment. Sometimes his mom had the stealth of a jungle cat. "What?"

"That she would be a good match for you," Colleen reminded him, inclining her head toward Lucy. "I still believe it."

"Not today Mom, okay?"

"Did you know that your dad was terrified of enclosed spaces and had night terrors?"

Brant snapped his gaze around. "What do you mean?"

"He fell down a mine shaft when he was eight years old. He was trapped there for two days. He used to wake up screaming some nights. Knowing he had fears, flaws…it didn't make me love him any less."

Brant's stomach dropped. "Mom, don't."

"The fact that he could admit it," she said pointedly. "That's what made him strong. And a better man for it. And it made me love him even more."

Brant watched Lucy wander by the stables as his mother spoke. He resisted the urge to join her, to hold her steady as she trudged over the thin blanket of snow, to keep her safe.

I've pretty much been in love with you since I was fifteen years old...

Lucy's words echoed in his head and then lodged in his chest. No one had ever uttered those words to him before…and certainly not with such heartbreaking honesty. But Lucy was always honest.

Right from the start she'd told him the truth. Right from the start she'd had a way of making him think and feel when he'd believed himself too numb to feel anything. The way she'd opened up about her own past had switched something on inside him. She had demons… regrets…but she'd forged ahead, carving out a successful career and becoming a kind, compassionate and considerate person. The best person he'd ever known. And she'd shared a part of herself with him so earnestly…so honestly. It wasn't just sex. Being with Lucy was like nothing he'd experienced before. Making love to her, feeling her touch, watching her come apart in his arms, was both spiritual and physical. The perfect moment. The perfect feeling. She was perfect.

"I know you were incredibly close to your uncle," his mother said quietly. "But don't go down the same lonely road that he did. When Joe came back from the war without one of his legs he thought he was somehow defined by that…so he never allowed himself to have a serious relationship with anyone. He never fell in love. He never had a family of his own. And I don't want the same thing to happen to you."

"It won't, Mom," he assured her. "I'm not an amputee for one—"

"Some wounds are on the outside, some are on the inside," she said with emphasis.

"She's right."

Grady's voice snapped his head around. His brother came up behind them and stood to Brant's left. Flanked by his mother and brother, he felt like he was suddenly in the center of an intervention. And in that moment all he wanted to do was to head down the stairs and find solace with Lucy. Looking at her walking through the snow alone made his insides ache. And the only thing that would appease that ache would be to be by her side... by sitting on the couch holding hands or watching football over cold pizza and beer. By kissing her beautiful mouth. By making love with her and feeling the tenderness of her touch. She was the tonic he needed. She was *all* he needed.

Brant stilled and every muscle in his body tightened.

He really needed her.

When he'd convinced himself he didn't need anything or anyone. Only solitude and time to dilute the pain and guilt that some days seemed etched into his very soul. And yet, Lucy knew that. She knew that and still wanted him. *Still loved him.* Because she was strong and courageous. She'd traveled her own road, recovering from the grief of losing her mother so tragically, and still found the strength and fortitude to allow someone into her heart. To allow *him* into her heart...even though he'd pushed her away again and again.

And he knew why.

Because he was scared. Terrified that he wouldn't measure up, that she'd think him weak, unworthy. That she would see him at his worst and still stay...out of loyalty. And pity. And that would be unbearable. He didn't want her sympathy. He didn't want her thinking she needed to fix him. He wanted to meet her head-on. Without fear.

Because...

Because he was in love with her. Wholly and completely.

Lucy Monero held every part of his heart and body and soul.

He watched her, a breathtaking vision in her red coat,

her head bent and her beautiful hair spilling out from beneath her hat. No one could ever come close. No one ever would.

Brant looked at his mother and then at Grady, and finally let out a long breath before speaking the words that were in his heart. "I'm in love with Lucy."

Grady laughed softly and his mother squeezed his arm. "Yes, we know," she said.

"The thing is," his brother said, still smiling, "what are you going to do about it?"

Brant looked toward the stables, watched her as she walked, his heart and mind filling with a kind of peace he'd never know before. "I'm going to ask her if she'll have me."

And he knew just how to do that.

Lucy was glad to be back at work. It was two days after Joe Parker's funeral and she was trying to get her life back into some kind of bearable rhythm. The hospital was busier than usual for a Wednesday, and since Christmas was only a couple of weeks away, there seemed to be an increase in the number of tourists coming into the ER with everything from stomach bugs to blisters. Lucy put on her best smile and spent the first few hours of her shift in Triage.

And she tried to *not* think about her broken heart.

It wasn't easy. Everything reminded her of Brant. Every time she walked into the ER she remembered him the afternoon his uncle had been brought in so many weeks ago, and how she'd quickly found herself in his relieved embrace. She couldn't walk through the front foyer without remembering how he'd brought her dinner on Thanksgiving. And at home the memories were even more intense. Sitting on the couch drinking beer and eating pizza, watching a silly football game together, making love as though there were no other people on earth. *Everything* reminded her of Brant. And her dreams offered no respite. He filled them, consumed them, and each morning she woke lethargic and with a heavy heart.

Kayla stopped by with lattes at lunchtime on Wednesday and Brooke called her after lunch to ensure she was okay. Ash came in around two o'clock to question a young man who'd been in a minor vehicular accident and had whiplash. She stayed to chat for a few minutes and Lucy tried to appear to be her usual happy self. She knew what her friends were doing and loved them for it…but mostly, she just wanted to be left alone.

There was nothing anyone could say or do to ease the ache in her heart and she didn't want to burden her friends with her unhappy mood. She'd get over it in her own time. Once she stopped thinking about Brant. And dreaming about him. Only then would she stop loving him.

She'd considered calling him several times in the past couple of days, but every time she grabbed her cell phone she simply stared at the screen. They had nothing to say to one another and no words were necessary. She knew how he felt. He couldn't give her what she wanted and she couldn't settle for anything less.

I just need some time to get over him.

But as she thought the words she didn't really believe them.

By three o'clock the flow of patients into the ER had eased. Lucy was about to make a final walk around the ward before she prepared to go home when she was paged. She answered the call and was asked to go down to the main reception area as there was someone waiting to see her. Thinking it was one of her friends again,

Lucy grabbed her white coat and slipped it on before she headed out through Triage and toward the front of the building. When she stepped out of the elevator she took a left turn and stopped in her tracks, suddenly poleaxed.

There were several people walking through the foyer, but she only saw one.

Brant...

He stood by the small bench seat where they had shared dinner from a basket and drank sodas. But this time he was dressed immaculately in a tuxedo and shiny black shoes and he carried a small, clear box with a flower inside.

Lucy stared at him, mesmerized. He looked so good. So handsome. His blue eyes glittered and his dark hair shone beneath the bright overhead lights. He didn't move and Lucy somehow found the strength to take a few steps toward him. Suddenly she didn't see anyone else or hear anyone else in the room. Only him.

Finally, he held out the small box and spoke.

"I just want you to know," he said, his deep voice like silk, "that you will always have a date for the prom."

Lucy's breath caught and tears instantly heated her eyes.

It was the single most beautiful, romantic moment of her life.

She wanted to race into his arms. But she held back. That had a lot to talk about. A lot to think about.

"Is…is that for me?" she asked.

He nodded. "Everything is for you, Lucia."

Lucy experienced an acute sense of joy and stepped a little closer. He was in front of her, dressed in a suit and holding a corsage, with his heart on his sleeve and no walls between them. And in that moment she had never loved him more.

"Brant..." Her words trailed off as emotion clogged her throat.

"Lucy," he said softly and held out his hand. "Is there somewhere we can talk in private?"

She nodded, took his hand and walked away from reception and up the corridor. There were several empty offices and she tapped on one of the doors and entered. If anyone walked by she didn't notice. She saw only him. She didn't care if anyone wondered why the most gorgeous man on the planet was doing with a harried-looking doctor wearing scrubs and a white coat.

The room was a small and perfunctory—typical of any administration office, with a desk, filing cabinet and two chairs. She closed the door and turned to face him. He held out the box again. She took it with trembling hands and looked at the perfect orchid corsage. "It's beautiful."

He held her hand tightly and nodded. "Shall we sit down?"

Lucy sat in one of the chairs and waited while he pulled the other one close. As soon as he sat he grabbed her free hand and spoke. "I know I've repeatedly screwed things up from the start. I know I've behaved badly. I know I've pushed you away time and time again. And I know I have no right to ask this of you...but I'm asking without any agenda, without any notion that I deserve it...but would you give me another chance?"

Her heart contracted and she smiled, seeing the love in his expression. He'd reached out in the most amazing way and she felt confident enough to meet him halfway, so she nodded. "Of course."

He looked instantly relieved. "Thank you. For believing in me. For understanding me. For having the patience to wait for me while I came to my senses."

Lucy smiled. "Have you? Come to your senses, I mean?"

He nodded. "Absolutely. I can't bear the thought of my life without you in it."

Lucy had never heard anything more heartfelt in her life. "I love you, too."

He kissed her then, a soft, slow kiss that kindled her longing for him. When he pulled back, his blue eyes were so vibrant she could almost see her reflection.

He held her hand lovingly. "What time do you finish today?"

Lucy checked her watch. It was two minutes to three. "Just about now."

"So," he said, curling a hand around her nape. "How about we get out of here and you go home and put on your prettiest dress and I'll take you out somewhere and we'll do this properly."

"Do what properly?" she teased.

"You know very well," he said and lovingly tucked a lock of stray hair behind her ear. "I'm not going to ask you to marry me while we're sitting in a hospital office room."

Lucy's heart almost exploded in her chest. "Oh… you're going to ask me to marry you?"

He smiled. "I most certainly am. But not here."

"Well," she said and leaned closer. "How about we go home and I won't put on my prettiest dress. Instead," she whispered, going closer still, "you can get out of that ridiculously sexy tuxedo and we can kiss and make up for a while and then you can ask me. Because I miss you. I miss *us*."

Brant kissed her softly and took the corsage box from her hand. He extracted the flower and carefully pinned it to her white coat. "I miss us, too."

She looked at the flower then met his gaze. "Brant what happened…what made you—?"

"What made me see sense?" he asked, cutting her off gently. He grabbed her hands and held them close. "What made me realize that I couldn't live without you? A few things. The other day my brother asked me what I was afraid of and I couldn't answer him. And then after the funeral, my mom told me not to end up like my uncle… because I had somehow come to think that my past is what defines me…and not my present. But I think…" he said, his words trailing for a moment as he softly touched her cheek. "I think that it was you. I *know* it was you. I was watching you walk alone in the snow the other day at the ranch, wearing your red coat… You looked so beautiful it took my breath away. But you looked alone, too. And that was unbearable for me. In that moment I knew… I just knew."

Lucy's eyes burned and she managed a quivering smile. "You knew what?"

He took a long breath. "I knew that I was in love with you."

They were the sweetest words she had ever heard. She reached up and cupped his smooth jaw. "I will always love you, Brant. And I'll always be there for you… through fire and rain…through bad dreams and sleepless nights."

His eyes glittered. "I wish I could tell you that I was through the worst of it, Lucy. But I can't."

She kept her hand against him. "You were in a war. And you experienced something life altering. You have to get through this at your own pace, Brant…but you also have to forgive yourself enough to let that happen. And that will take time. And patience. And probably therapy.

But there are no judges, no one here to devalue your feelings. There's just you…and me."

He groaned softly and captured her mouth in a kiss. "I love you, Lucia," he said against her lips. "I love your strength and your goodness. I love how you make the most of every moment. And I'm humbled that you want to love me back. There's no one in the world like you," he said and smiled, love in his eyes. "And I will love you and protect you and honor you always."

Lucy's throat burned with emotion. He was such a passionate, strong yet gentle man. And knowing she had his love filled her heart with overwhelming happiness. She knew they had some hurdles ahead, but Lucy was confident they would get through it together.

"So, about this tuxedo," she said and toyed with the bow tie. "Although it looks great on you, I still like the idea about going home and getting out of these clothes. And you did promise me a proposal, remember?"

He laughed softly and pulled her onto his lap. "I certainly did. Speaking of homes, in a few weeks I'm going to be homeless. The new chef is taking over the apartment above the tavern," he explained. "So unless you want to see me out on the street, I might have to bunk at your place for a while."

Lucy smiled and pressed kissed to his jaw. "Oh, I think we could come to some arrangement." Her eyes sparkled. "But that means sleepovers, you know. Cold sweats and bad dreams and all."

"I know what it means," he said as his arms tightened around her. "And although I'm probably going to struggle at first with you seeing me like that, I know I need to let go of the fear that you'll think I'm…needy…and weak."

"You don't have a weak bone in your body, Brant Parker," she said, her heart aching for him. "But I understand. And we'll simply take it one day, and one night, at a time."

He nodded slowly. "Dr. Allenby was telling me about the group therapy sessions they hold at the veterans home, you know, for the veterans and their families." He squeezed her hand. "I was wondering if you'd come with me sometime."

"Of course," she said quickly. "Of course I'll come with you. From this moment I don't ever want to be apart from you."

"Me, either."

She pressed against him. "And I love the idea of us living together."

"Me, too." He held her close. "Let's get out of here, Lucy. Let's go home so I can get down on my knee and ask you to marry me."

Lucy smiled cheekily. "Do you have a ring?"

His eyes darkened. "Of course."

"Then I accept!"

He laughed and the lovely sound reverberated through her entire body. "I haven't technically asked you yet."

"That's true," she said quickly and jumped to her feet. "Then let's go. I don't want you changing your mind about this."

Brant stood and hauled her into his arms. "Just so you know, Lucia, I will never change my mind. You're stuck with me for the rest of your life."

And that, Lucy thought as she offered her lips for his kiss, was the best news she'd ever heard.

Epilogue

"You know, you can protest all you like, but I *am* going to carry you over this threshold."

Lucy stared up at him, all green eyes and red lips. "But it's bad luck if we're not married."

Brant shook his head. "We're getting married in nine weeks. A date that *you* set, if you remember," he reminded her. "*I* would have happily eloped over Christmas."

"If we eloped, your mother would never forgive us," she said and crossed her arms. "Nor your brother or Kayla or Ash or Brooke."

She was right, of course. Eloping had never been an option. And she was right to suggest a six-month engagement. They needed time to get to know one another better, for Brant to continue with his sessions with Dr. Allenby, to arrange a wedding and to buy a house. Which is why they were now standing on the porch of their new home and she was being typically stubborn about his insistence he carry her over the threshold.

"Well, I have these," he said and dangled the keys from his fingertips. "So, I either carry you or we stay out here."

She glared at him. "You can been a real pain sometimes."

He shrugged. "I thought you found me charming?"

Her glare quickly turned into a smile. "Yeah… I do."

Brant laughed. "Well, climb the steps and come here."

She trudged up the five steps onto the porch. "This is really silly. What if someone sees us?"

"Some like who?"

She shrugged. "Our new neighbors perhaps."

He looked left and then right. "Old Mrs. Bailey plays bridge on Thursdays and is out, and the other side is Joss Culhane's house. Which you know. So, stop making excuses and get over here."

She chuckled and the sound hit him directly in the heart. Everything about her made him smile. Lucy was an amazing woman—kind, considerate, supportive and a tower of strength. Much more than he deserved, he was sure. But she loved him and he loved her in return, more than he'd ever imagined he could love anyone.

The past three months had been something of a whirlwind. With planning a wedding, opening the tavern, taking a part-time job teaching French at the high school and buying a home, there never seemed enough hours in the day. But Lucy was always at his side and unfailing in her support. She always made time to accompany him to the group meetings at the veterans home and had been with him in several of his sessions with Dr. Allenby. She'd been right about that, too. Time was a healer. Truth was a healer. He'd discovered both those things with her love and support. He'd even begun sleeping through the night.

The nightmares still came, but he was better prepared to handle them. And he'd forgiven himself, finally, for surviving the war when so many people around him hadn't.

"Where do you want me?" she asked, standing beside him.

Brant opened the security screen and then the front door. The house was big, low set and had been freshly renovated by the previous owners. Exactly what they wanted. Three bedrooms, two bathrooms, a huge kitchen and dining area, a large living room and a yard that needed a little work. But he didn't mind. Seeing Lucy's delighted expression the first time they'd viewed the house was enough to ensure he'd made an offer to the Realtor on the spot.

"I want you right here," he said and held out his arms. He scooped her up and jiggled her playfully. "Hmm… you're heavier than I thought."

She scowled and tapped him on the shoulder. "That's not very—"

"I'm kidding," he said and crossed the threshold. "You're as light as a feather."

She smiled and he carried her down the hall toward the kitchen. Since there was no furniture in the house, he propped her on the Canadian maple countertop and she smoothed her skirt down over her thighs. He kissed her cheek and then waved an arm to the middle of the dining area.

"We need to buy a new table," he said.

"My furniture arrives tomorrow," she reminded him. "Let's get it in the house and then see what we need."

He grinned. "My logical love."

She nodded and met his gaze. "While we're on that subject… I was thinking it would be logical to move the wedding up a bit. Say, to April."

Brant frowned slightly. "April? That's next month. Why would you want to do that when everything's booked for June?"

He looked at her and realized she seemed on edge. Even nervous. It occurred to him that she'd been a little distracted for days. Now he was really concerned. He said her name and she sighed heavily.

"I just want to make sure," she said softly.

"Make sure of what?"

"That I still fit into my wedding dress."

Brant stilled instantly. Her dress? He met her gaze and saw her expression change. Now she was smiling, a kind of delighted, secret smile that reached him way down. And she deliberately lay a palm on her belly.

Her belly…

A strange sensation tightened his throat as his gaze flicked from her eyes to where her hand lay. And in an instant he knew. "Are you pregnant?"

She nodded. "Sure am."

Emotion rose and hit him square in the middle of the chest. Pregnant. A baby. A dad.

And Brant didn't know whether he wanted to laugh, cry or pass out.

Lucy couldn't help smiling at the look on his face. She'd kept the secret for two days, wanting to break the news in their new home…for a new beginning…a new chapter in their life together.

"Are you okay, Brant?" she asked, taking in his sudden pallor.

"I…think so. Are you sure?"

She nodded. "Positive."

He took two steps across the room and settled between her thighs, hugging her tightly. "How far along?"

"About six weeks."

She could see him doing the math calculation in his head. "The night of the opening?"

"Yes," she replied, remembering how the night of the Loose Moose reopening they'd celebrated a little too hard and forgotten contraception. They'd joked about it at the time. Now, Lucy couldn't be more delighted that they'd neglected to use protection that night. She was over the moon, happier than she'd ever been in her life. Having Brant's baby was a dream come true. "Are you in shock?"

"A little," he admitted. "You?"

"I've had two days to get used to the idea," she said and smiled. "But I wanted to tell you here…in this house. *Our house.*"

He kissed her, long and passionately and filled with love.

"I'm gonna be a dad? Really?"

"Really," she replied.

He kissed her softly. "I can't believe how lucky I am. I can't believe I have all this. That I have you. And now…" He looked down at her belly. "And now we're having a baby together…it's as though suddenly I have this perfect life."

Lucy grabbed his hand and laid it against her stomach. "We do," she assured him and saw his eyes glittering with emotion. Lucy touched his face. "And you're going to be great. *We're* going to be great. Everything *is* going to be perfect, Brant."

When their beautiful son, Joel, was born a little more than seven months later, everything was perfect, just as she'd known it would be.

* * * * *

Don't miss Brooke Laughton's story,
THE COWGIRL'S FOREVER FAMILY,
the next installment of Helen Lacey's new miniseries,
THE CEDAR RIVER COWBOYS
On sale September 2016
wherever Harlequin books and ebooks are sold.

Available June 21, 2016

#2485 MARRIAGE, MAVERICK STYLE!

Montana Mavericks: The Baby Bonanza • by Christine Rimmer

Tessa Strickland is *done* with hotshot men like billionaire Carson Drake. But after they wake up together following the Rust Creek Falls Baby Parade, Carson isn't willing to let the brunette beauty go without a fight. Especially when they might have their own baby bonanza from that night they don't quite remember...

#2486 THE BFF BRIDE

Return to the Double C • by Allison Leigh

Brilliant scientist Justin Clay and diner manager Tabby Taggart were best friends for decades, until one night of passion ruined everything. Now Justin is back in Weaver for work, and Tabby can't seem to stop running into him at every turn. With their "just friends" front crumbling, Justin must realize all the success he's dreamed of doesn't mean much without the girl he's always loved.

#2487 THIRD TIME'S THE BRIDE!

Three Coins in the Fountain • by Merline Lovelace

Dawn McGill has left two fiancés at the altar already, terrified her marriage will turn as bitter as her parents'. CEO Brian Ellis is wary of Dawn's past when he hires her as a nanny, not wanting his son to suffer another loss after the death of his mother. But Brian can't help the growing attraction he feels to the vibrant redhead. Is the third time really the charm for these two lonely hearts?

#2488 PUPPY LOVE FOR THE VETERINARIAN

Peach Leaf, Texas • by Amy Woods

A freak snowstorm leaves June Leavy and the puppies she rescued stranded at the Peach Leaf veterinary office, forcing her to spend the night there with Ethan Singh. Bad breakups have burned them both, leaving them with scars and shattered dreams. They're determined to find homes for the puppies, but can they find a home with each other along the way?

#2489 THE MATCHMAKING TWINS

Sugar Falls, Idaho • by Christy Jeffries

The Gregson twins long for a new mommy. So when they overhear their father, former navy SEAL captain Luke Gregson, admit to an attraction to their favorite local cop, Carmen Delgado, they come up with a plan to throw the two adults together. But will the grown-ups see beyond their painful pasts to a new chance at love and a family?

#2490 HIS SURPRISE SON

The Men of Thunder Ridge • by Wendy Warren

Golden boy Nate Thayer returns home to discover that time hasn't dimmed his desire for Izzy Lambert, the girl he once loved and lost. But can Izzy, a girl from the wrong side of the tracks, trust that this time Nate is here to stay...especially when he discovers the secret she's been keeping for years?

YOU CAN FIND MORE INFORMATION ON UPCOMING HARLEQUIN® TITLES, FREE EXCERPTS AND MORE AT WWW.HARLEQUIN.COM.

HSECNM0616

After a night under the influence of Homer Gilmore's infamous moonshine, Tessa Strickland and Carson Drake decide to take it slow, but these two commitmentphobes might be in for the surprise of their lives...

Read on for a sneak preview of MARRIAGE, MAVERICK STYLE!, the first installment of the new miniseries, ***MONTANA MAVERICKS: THE BABY BONANZA****, by* New York Times *bestselling author Christine Rimmer.*

He resisted the urge to tip up her chin and make her meet his eyes again. "So you're not mad at me for moving in here?"

And then she did look at him. God. He wished she would never look away. "No, Carson. I'm not mad. How long are you staying?"

"Till the nineteenth. I have meetings in LA the week of the twentieth."

She touched him then, just a quick brush of her hand on the bare skin of his forearm. Heat curled inside him, and he could have sworn that actual sparks flashed from the point of contact. Then she confessed, her voice barely a whisper, "I regretted saying goodbye to you almost from the moment I hung up the phone yesterday."

"Good." The word sounded rough to his own ears. "Because I'm going nowhere for the next two weeks."

She slanted him a sideways glance. "You mean that I'm getting a second chance with you whether I want one or not?"

All possible answers seemed dangerous. He settled on "Yes."

HSEEXP0616

"I... Um. I want to take it slow, Carson. I want to..." She glanced down—and then up to meet his eyes full-on again. "Don't laugh."

He banished the smile that was trying to pull at his mouth. "I'm not laughing."

"I want to be friends with you. Friends first. And then we'll see."

Friends. Not really what he was going for. He wanted so much more. He wanted it all—everything that had happened Monday night that he couldn't remember. He wanted her naked, pressed tight against him. Wanted to coil that wild, dark hair around his hand, kiss her breathless, bury himself to the hilt in that tight, pretty body of hers, make her beg him to go deeper, hear her cry out his name.

But none of that was happening right now. So he said the only thing he could say, given the circumstances. "However you want it, Tessa."

"You're sure about that?"

"I am."

"Because I'm..." She ran out of steam. Or maybe courage.

And that time he did reach out to curl a finger beneath her chin. She resisted at first, but then she gave in and lifted her gaze to his once more. He asked, "You're what?"

"I'm not good at this, you know?" She stared at him, her mouth soft and pliant, all earnestness, so sweetly sincere. "I'm kind of a doofus when it comes to romance and all that."